'Was that who I think it was on your doorstep this morning, Simon?'

He plunged. 'It was Morwenna Barker. She's come to work for me.'

Little Simms chuckled. 'You're a dark horse, Simon!'

Burrows, judicial as ever, came in last. 'Was it your idea?'

'No. She turned up yesterday afternoon and asked for the job. What could I do?'

Burrows nodded, 'I see that, but you should ask yourself what she's up to. The Barkers never do anything without a reason and in this case it can't be money, not on what you'll pay her.' A pause for consideration, then the diagnosis. 'If you ask me, there's more in this than meets the eye.'

Simon did not need to be told that a large stone had been dropped into his small pond.

W.J. Burley lived near Newquay in Cornwall, and was a schoolmaster until he retired to concentrate on his writing. His many Wycliffe books include, most recently, *Wycliffe and the Guild of Nine*. He died in 2002.

By *W.J. Burley*

WYCLIFFE SERIES
Wycliffe and the Three-Toed Pussy
Wycliffe and How to Kill a Cat
Wycliffe and the Guilt Edged Alibi
Wycliffe and Death in a Salubrious Place
Wycliffe and Death in Stanley Street
Wycliffe and the Pea-Green Boat
Wycliffe and the School Bullies
Wycliffe and the Scapegoat
Wycliffe in Paul's Court
Wycliffe's Wild-Goose Chase
Wycliffe and the Beales
Wycliffe and the Four Jacks
Wycliffe and the Quiet Virgin
Wycliffe and the Winsor Blue
Wycliffe and the Tangled Web
Wycliffe and the Cycle of Death
Wycliffe and the Dead Flautist
Wycliffe and the Last Rites
Wycliffe and the Dunes Mystery
Wycliffe and the House of Fear
Wycliffe and the Redhead
Wycliffe and the Guild of Nine

HENRY PYM SERIES
A Taste of Power
Death in Willow Pattern

OTHER NOVELS
The Schoolmaster
The Sixth Day
Charles and Elizabeth
The House of Care

Wycliffe
AND THE
REDHEAD

W.J.Burley

An Orion paperback

First published in Great Britain in 1997
by Victor Gollancz Ltd
Published in paperback in 1998
by Corgi
This paperback edition published in 2007
by Orion Books Ltd,
Orion House, 5 Upper St Martin's Lane,
London WC2H 9EA

An Hachette UK company

3 5 7 9 10 8 6 4 2

ISBN 978–0–7528–8143–0

Printed and bound in Great Britain by
Clays Ltd, St Ives plc

The Orion Publishing Group's policy is to use papers that
are natural, renewable and recyclable products and
made from wood grown in sustainable forests. The logging
and manufacturing processes are expected to conform to
the environmental regulations of the country of origin.

www.orionbooks.co.uk

Wycliffe

AND THE

REDHEAD

Chapter One

A winter's morning. Simon opened his eyes and saw the dim outline of his dormer window against the dawn. He sat up in bed, pushed aside the grey blankets and put his feet over the side, feeling for his slippers.

A day like any other.

He slouched across to the window. His attic room was higher than the pub opposite and looking across a landscape of roofs he could glimpse in the far distance a ribbon of sea.

Half-past seven. A cold raw day and he was late.

The little attic was cheerless, the furniture eclectic and basic: a single iron bedstead, a chest, a table, a few rickety bookshelves, an armchair losing its stuffing and a gas fire fitted into a cast iron mantelpiece, painted brown.

Simon Meagor, antiquarian bookseller.

Simon, carrying his clothes, clopped down steep stairs to the floor below and into a different world. The corridor was carpeted; white-painted doors opened off on either side and each door had a little enamelled label with a flowery motif: Rebecca,

Jonathan, Bathroom, Toilet, Mum and Dad, Living Room, Kitchen.

All this from the time when Judith believed that with enthusiasm, organization and an uncharacteristic touch of whimsy she could domesticate her husband and make the marriage work. It was now ten years since she left, taking the children with her, and only this material evidence remained as testimony to her efforts.

Simon went into the bathroom. He washed, shaved and brushed his teeth. His movements were heavy and slow; he was a big man, with bone, muscle and sinew to match.

With a slightly bemused expression he studied himself in the mirror. His features were large, his forehead broad, and his grey eyes were set wide apart. Yet there was a softness, a vagueness of expression, out of keeping with the rest. His thick, curly, greying hair fitted like a cap.

For as long as he could remember, mirrors had held for Simon a disturbing fascination. He distrusted that looking-glass world and he would sometimes ask himself, Is that man in the glass really Simon Meagor? Is that man who looks so solid and predictable, *me*?

For Simon's life was slipping by, and he was drifting. He would continue in a state of mild anaesthesia for days at a time, and though his occasional encounters with reality were rarely pleasant, it troubled him.

In the little kitchen, where the gas cooker, in common with the rest, could have done with a good clean, he fed his cat, Lady Lu, and prepared his own breakfast. A boiled egg and two pieces of toast were followed by three cups of coffee. As he ate, he read from a volume of André Gide's journal, but it could have been from almost any diary, journal or biography taken at random from the shelves downstairs.

Simon's routine was fixed, and he found it hard to believe that he had once been a married man. Those years when he had shared the flat with a woman and their children were unreal; they had the quality of a dream. The children were grown-up: Rebecca was twenty-two, Jonathan, nineteen. They lived with their mother in the town, and from time to time one or other of them would drop in to see him; amiable, neutral.

At five minutes to nine, followed by Lady Lu, Simon went downstairs to his office, a small space at the back of the shop. It looked out on his yard and on the blank wall of the market house. He opened the door for Lady Lu to go out.

His shop was one of a pair in narrow, crooked Moor Street. Each had well-worn granite steps to its door and a bulging Dickensian window of small panes.

Simon's neighbour dealt in old china and glass. Between the two shops an alley led to a covered market of fifty stalls, selling everything from vegetables to videos.

Simon switched on the lights, bringing to dusty life the rows of bookshelves which ran the length of the shop to the window on the street. Unhurried, he made his way along one of the aisles, pausing now and then to restore a stray book to its proper place or merely to touch, almost to caress, a particular favourite.

Simon sold second-hand books which, for the most part, were of the up-market kind, classed as antiquarian. But at heart he was a collector, and too often he was faced with the decision whether to sell or to keep.

He unlocked the shop door, changed the notice from 'Closed' to 'Open' and collected his mail from the wire basket. Outside it was drizzling rain and there was condensation inside the shop window.

On the other side of the market entrance Jeremy Scott of the china shop went through the same ritual. Jerry was short and stout with a high colour and a wispy moustache; a widower, looked after by his daughter. They exchanged greetings by gesture.

Because of the damaging effects of sunlight there were no books in Simon's window, but there was a printed card which read: 'Assistant wanted. Apply within.'

There had been no suitable applicants and the sign had been there for so long he had almost forgotten about it.

Simon set about sorting through a parcel of books, the result of his telephone bids at a recent auction. People wandered in and out of the shop and he made the occasional sale, but for the most part they were browsers. Some needed watching. Rarely, a book was stolen; the greater risk was defacement by the removal of an eye-catching print.

He regarded these auction parcels as lucky dips. He examined each book, assessing it for condition and quality, deciding on the appropriate mark-up, and came at the last to a mid-nineteenth-century travel book, part of a random lot. He turned the pages idly: several good maps, some passable illustrations; nothing to make a fuss about, but the book was saleable.

The fly leaf had stuck lightly to the cover and it was only when he separated them that he found the inscription:

To Dear Baby, Her Royal Highness Princess Beatrice, on her sixteenth birthday, from Mother. Osborne. April 16th 1873.

Somebody had slipped up, and he felt like a punter who has brought off a modest double.

At half-past ten he went to join a small group of familiars in the market café, but not until he had displayed the usual notice inside the glass of his shop door: 'Back in fifteen minutes'.

The café tables were set out at the very hub of the market, under the glass roof, and people milled around, moving slowly along the aisles or lingering at the stalls.

Three regulars beside himself shared a table: Jeremy Scott from next door; little Colin Simms, bald-headed and monkey-faced, from costume jewellery and Korean watches; and Eddie Burrows from fruit and vegetables, making this routine escape from his wife.

Burrows was tall, cadaverous and rheumy-eyed, with a morose disposition. His sole pleasure in life seemed to lie in being first with bad news.

As soon as the fat woman had served Simon with his mug of coffee and chocolate biscuit, Burrows fixed him with a stare that was almost accusing. 'I suppose you've heard that Nicky Barker's back in town? . . . Saw him in the Queen's last night. They say he's shacked up with the Pardon boy and a girl, sharing a squat in Carver's Ope.'

Jeremy Scott sipped his coffee, apparently unaware

that it was dripping on to his woolly cardigan. He wiped his moustache and ruminated. 'Nicky Barker. That sister of his must still be around somewhere – Morwenna, that's what they called her. Funny sort of name, but she was a fine-looking young piece. I've always fancied redheads. Hard to believe she and Nicky were peas out of the same pod.'

Burrows, ever ready for contention, said, 'They weren't. You've got it wrong, Jerry. Morwenna was Nicky's cousin. Her father took Nicky in when he was orphaned in that car crash, but the boy was a layabout and it didn't last.' He turned to Meagor. 'Isn't that right, Simon?'

Simon, looking down at his half-eaten biscuit, muttered inaudibly.

Burrows put on a show of puzzlement. 'Why get so uptight, Simon, when anybody mentions the Barkers? I mean, everybody knows it was you who put their old man away, but you was only doing your duty. You just stood up in court and told 'em what you saw an' what you heard. Isn't that right?'

Simon said nothing. In his mind's eye he was seeing a man, prone on a tiled floor, his head in a pool of blood.

Colin Simms, the little jeweller, changed the subject, but Simon's day, which had started well, was already spoiled.

That night, in a students hostel on the outskirts of Camborne, Morwenna Barker was asleep and dreaming, a nightmare dream. She was lying on her back, unable to move, and a man was bending over her. She could just see him in the dim light. His face was very thin and white, and he was quite bald except for a white fringe above the ears. He reminded her of her neurologist, but there was a satanic twist to his features, and he spoke in a harsh whisper.

'I think you know, Miss . . . ah . . . Barker, that the news is not good. You have multiple sclerosis – mul-ti-ple scler-os-is – and that means you are dying, dy-ing . . .' His whispers seemed to echo through cavernous gloom. 'You are slow-ly dy-ing.'

Morwenna woke, trembling, her heart pounding, unsure whether or not she had let out a cry.

The curtains were undrawn and the window framed a starlit sky. The pale light reflected dimly from the mirror over her dressing table. The luminous dial of her little clock showed a quarter-past two. Nothing had changed. The world was indifferent.

The pain was behind her right eye and there was a slight numbness in her right hand.

Morwenna twisted violently on to her side, taking the bedclothes with her, and muttered, 'I'll think about nothing. I'll concentrate on a large empty space.'

But vivid little cameos presented themselves to her mind, like images flashed on a screen, then snatched away.

Her father, being cross-examined by counsel, bewildered, and allowing himself to be tied in knots.

Her father in prison, thinner, grey-faced, adrift, striving to summon up some semblance of warmth; trying to smile . . .

Her father, having joined them as a tolerated guest of her aunt, trying his best to appear relaxed and normal, but behaving like a man lost.

Her father, in the bath, fully clothed, blood every-where.

Her mother . . .

And above all, Simon Meagor in the witness box – lying!

She slept at last, and woke in the first grey light of dawn. Half-past seven by her little clock. Drizzling rain blew fitfully against her window.

Brushing her hair, she too studied her reflection in the mirror. She saw red hair cascading to bare shoulders; a pale face, lightly freckled; and blue eyes that were brooding and intent.

It seems not so very long ago that I used to wonder what I would do with my life. I tried to imagine what it would be like to live with a man, to sleep with him on a regular basis, perhaps to have his child and be a mother. I also considered going to university and making a career. In fact, there seemed no reason why I shouldn't do both.

But that was when I had a future. Or thought I had.

Now in my mirror I see grubby sheets on a tumbled bed, yellowing wallpaper that has lost its pattern, a framed print of some anonymous beach and a few books on an improvised shelf.

That is my room in this place. But do I want to put myself to the trouble of changing it – or anything?

A rat-tat on her door. 'It's half-eight, Wenna, love! . . . Bathroom's free, if you're quick.' Debbie, her landlady.

Morwenna lodged in a hostel with students from the college where she worked as a librarian. Downstairs a dozen girls, all several years younger than she, chattered over their coffee, cornflakes and toast.

A few years earlier she could have been one of them.

She drank a cup of coffee and hurried out of the house, to drive off in her little buttercup-yellow Mini to the college library.

Debbie, motherly, saw her off. 'You're heading for trouble if you go on like this, love.'

Morwenna murmured, 'I don't have to head for it; I'm in it.'

As she drove she thought, Friday. Saturday tomorrow. The interminable weekend. I shall read and brood in my room. I shall go for walks to kill time. I shall go to bed early, and not sleep. I shall lie awake wondering if the numbness is coming back, whether there is really a pain behind my eye or if it's only my imagination. At worst, Matthew will come and it will start all over again.

She arrived at the college and parked between the white lines in a section reserved for the staff.

Saturday. A morning of leaden skies and unremitting rain, but business was brisk in the bookshop. Simon had a reputation among specialists and on Saturday mornings a sprinkling of bibliophiles browsed in the aisles between the rows of shelves. Simon circulated discreetly. He knew most of them; a word of greeting here, a suggestion there, a question answered.

It was in one of the aisles that he came across Nicky Barker standing, hands in pockets, looking like a predatory cat amongst unwary pigeons.

An exaggerated stage whisper: 'Hi, Simon! Long time no see. Business pretty good, eh?'

'You want to talk to me?'

'That was the idea.'

Simon led the way down the shop to his office.

Barker sat down without being invited. 'Things are a bit tight with me at the moment, Simon; so I thought it was time to get back home, like. Renew old acquaintances.'

Barker had changed, though not beyond recognition. His straight black hair, hanging limply to his shoulders, accentuated his long, thin, pale face. He was dressed wholly in black, with a frilly shirt and skin-tight jeans. He looked like the villainous doctor from some sci-fi epic.

Simon was nervous and showed it. 'What do you want?'

Barker's manner was relaxed, conversational, 'Well, first, I wondered if you'd seen anything of Morwenna. I'd like to make contact. After all, she's my cousin and blood's thicker than water. That's what they say, anyway.'

'No, I haven't seen Morwenna and I have no idea where she is.'

'Pity! Well, there was another thing. Seeing what happened to Uncle and all that, I thought a few quid now and then could be reasonable. Until I get on my feet.'

'As far as your uncle is concerned, I did only what I believed to be right at the time. I owe you nothing.'

'Who said anything about owing? The old man and I didn't get on but he was the nearest thing I had to a father and he would have helped me out of a hole when I needed it. Thanks to you, he's no longer with us, so I thought you might act in *loco parentis* so to speak.' A broad grin.

'You'll get nothing out of me.'

Barker looked hurt. 'That's a pity!' He moved his hand across the desk, sweeping three or four books to the floor. 'Sorry! I'll pick 'em up. I'm real sorry about that, but I get clumsy when I'm upset. And it's funny, but I've got friends who are just like me.'

Barker got up to go. Simon, trembling with anger, but scared, followed him, and saw him off at the shop door. A few yards down the street Barker turned to say, 'See you around, Simon!'

On that same Saturday morning, shortly after returning to her room from breakfast, Morwenna heard a tap on her door. 'Who is it?'

'Me.' The door opened and a young man came in; late teens, early twenties.

'Matthew!'

'I knew you wouldn't have gone out in this weather, so I came here. I thought we could talk.'

Matthew was tall and thin; blond with blue eyes, and an air of troubled innocence.

Morwenna was irritated, as much by his meekness as anything else. 'I told you I didn't want to see you any more. I meant it, Matthew. I don't want to talk to you here or anywhere. Do you understand?'

'You wanted me before you were ill, Wenna, and I wanted you. As far as I'm concerned nothing has changed.'

'No? I'm glad!' Morwenna was acid. 'Well, let me tell you, things have changed a hell of a lot for me.'

The boy flushed. 'I didn't mean that, Wenna. It was a stupid thing to say. What I meant was that we can face things together. I want to, and we must. After all, there's our baby—'

'What baby?'

'You told me—'

Morwenna snapped. 'That's all over. Did you think that with what I've got in front of me I was going to saddle myself with a kid? I've had an abortion, a termination. Our baby, as you call it, has gone down the pan.'

She had chosen her words with the deliberate intention of shocking, more accurately perhaps, of alienating him.

Matthew sat on the bed, his lips trembling, close to tears. For a moment he could not speak, then in a low pleading voice he said, 'Don't talk like that, Wenna! . . . don't, please!'

She realized that she had gone further than she had meant to do. She allowed the silence to build; then in her more normal voice, her manner apparently relaxed, she asked, 'How are they?'

Matthew gathered his wits. 'Much the same. They're both worried about you—'

'You haven't told them that I've got MS?'

'No, but I think you should. Mother would come and see you but she can't leave your aunt for long. They want you to come home, Wenna.'

'Yes, well, they don't know what they would be letting themselves in for, and neither do you.'

He went at last. She allowed him a peck on her cheek and he stood in the doorway looking back, doe-eyed, before closing the door.

She heard him going down the stairs and she heard Debbie quizzing him in the hall, then the front door slammed.

She threw herself on the bed and wept.

But on Sunday morning the sun was shining and there was a promise of spring. At rare intervals during the past six years Morwenna had sought to recover something of her childhood by revisiting the places she had known, and the house where she was born and brought up.

Even the air seemed different. For the first time in months she felt that there might be not a chance to begin again, but the possibility of finding a new direction.

She set out, pushing the little Mini hard, travelling south-eastwards across the narrow neck of the county through a lacework of unlikely lanes. Untroubled by conflicting fingerposts and outlandish names she arrived at last on what had once been her home ground.

A strange countryside to the north of the Helford River: moorland, criss-crossed by fertile valleys, pockmarked by quarries and scattered with strange cairns of weathering, discarded granite boulders.

And there was the house, tucked into the hillside overlooking the valley. 'Chygwyn', the White House, though it had never been white in living memory. She pulled off the road just below, so that she could look up at it.

Through some odd quirk of the mind she was distressed to see a 'For Sale' notice on a pole propped drunkenly by the gate. And those windows, three up and two down, were uncurtained. They looked out, unseeing, over a view that had become part of her psyche.

The notice said: 'Viewing by appointment only'.

On her last visit the house had been occupied; a woman was clipping the hedge and children were playing in the garden. Total strangers, but confirmation that life goes on. Now the hedge was ragged, the garden her father had made was overgrown, and the short gravelled drive was peppered with weeds.

She was on the point of driving away, seat-belt refastened, ignition key between finger and thumb. But she changed her mind. I won't pass up this chance to see the old house at close quarters.

She got out, crossed the road and entered the drive by the wicket gate, the gate she had 'helped' her father to make. She remembered that evening; she must have been seven or eight. There was a wooden tray with all sorts of screws in different compartments.

'No, not those, Wenna; we use brass screws for outdoors; they don't rust.'

Now, feeling like an intruder, she made for the back of the house where she could not be seen from the road. The yard, with its paving of granite slabs, was unchanged, and the little edifice which had once been an outside loo was still there. So were the steps leading up to her mother's vegetable patch. But the greenhouse was missing several panes . . .

Morwenna peered through the window into the large room they had called the dining room, where they had done most of their living. It looked cavernous and empty. The open wood-burning grate which had made it cosy in winter had been displaced by an electric heater.

In one of those borrowed moments, she saw it as it had been: the wood fire blazing; the black logs turning first to orange, then to a fierce yellow, almost white at the heart. She seemed to hear that crackle that would send sparks flying up the chimney.

And there was Morwenna sprawled on the hearth rug, turning the pages of a picture book. In the background her mother, a shadowy figure, statuesque and remote, was saying, 'Not too close to the fire, now!'

'Oh, I'm sorry. I hope I didn't startle you.'

Morwenna's day-dream ended. There was a man standing close to her, a youngish man, a strange figure with a clumsy, lop-sided body.

Morwenna, momentarily both startled and scared, was unreasonably reassured by a cultured voice and a pleasant manner.

'I really am sorry, but I came upon you unawares. Are you interested in the house?' Conversational.

'I was born and grew up here.'

'Really?' Morwenna told herself that his interest could hardly be as great as it sounded, but he went on, 'Then you must be a Barker. Your father was a builder.'

'And you? Should I know you?'

'I live at Polwheveral. My name is Cross – you may remember my father. Does the name "Doctor Cross" ring a bell?'

Light dawned on Morwenna. 'I do remember a Doctor Cross. He had a son . . .' She broke off, embarrassed.

An odd little smile. 'A son who was crippled. Quite right! Known to all but seen by few.'

'I'm sorry.'

'No need to be. I'm Julian.'

'Morwenna.'

As they walked away from the house Morwenna had a strange, irrational feeling that her life was about to change.

Julian's car, an Escort, was parked a little way down the hill. They were on the point of separating when he said, 'I thought of taking a walk; I don't suppose you would care to keep me company?'

Julian used a stick, and his right boot had a thick sole to compensate for the shortness of his right leg, but he covered the ground without apparent difficulty. They walked among the disused quarries, ignoring the 'Keep Out' signs.

At one point they were standing on the edge of a quarry, hewn out from the hillside in a great crescent. The quarry had flooded, and they were looking down on a body of water, a lake, embraced by the arms of the crescent, more than a hundred feet below.

Morwenna said, 'Job's Pit. I don't know who Job was unless it comes from the Bible. As children we used to come to the pool to sail toy boats. Some of the older boys used to swim, but the water was too cold.'

By the time they returned to their cars Morwenna had accepted an invitation for the next Saturday.

'Ventonbos, on the west side of the creek.'

'I'll find it.'

Chapter Two

On a Wednesday in late February Simon had just reopened the shop after lunch and he was at the office end pricing a parcel of books that had arrived that morning. Customers were few on Wednesdays and it was with a touch of surprise that he heard the door bell, followed by footsteps in one of the aisles. He looked up.

'Remember me?'

A young woman with red hair down her back; she wore a short waterproof jacket over a jade-green frock of fine clinging wool.

He looked at her foolishly. 'Morwenna!'

In that instant he was back in the courtroom and the judge was saying, 'Do you find the defendant guilty or not guilty?'

'Guilty.'

As sentence was being pronounced Simon was not looking at the judge, neither was the girl in the gallery, the girl with red hair. They were looking at each other and her expression had troubled him ever since. Disbelief? Contempt? Hatred?

He blundered on, 'You haven't changed . . .'

A half smile. 'In six years? Anyway, a lot has happened in that time. Mother and I went to live with Aunt Molly in St Ives; Father joined us when he had served his sentence – and killed himself shortly afterwards.'

Only her eyes belied her matter-of-fact, almost casual recital. 'Mother was devastated, and a year later she died of a heart attack.'

All Simon could find to say was, 'I'm sorry.'

A small dismissive gesture, then, 'But all that is in the past and I've come to Falmouth to make a fresh start. For the moment I'm lodging with the Burtons on the Bar but I shall be looking for somewhere more permanent.'

Still he could think of nothing to say.

She moved closer to the desk, pulled up a chair and sat down. 'You don't mind?'

'No – no!'

'You've got a card in the window; I've come for the job.'

'The job!' He could not believe that she was serious. 'You mean you want to work here?'

'That's what I said.'

'But you don't even know what the job is.'

'I know about books; I've worked in a library. I can type, and I can use a computer if you've got one. I'll soon learn how to talk to customers; I've had enough experience dealing with students.'

Simon clutched at straws. 'I couldn't pay you very much.'

'Pay me what you can to start, then you can make up your mind what I'm worth to the business. You've nothing to lose.'

Simon was desperate. 'But I mean, there's what happened . . .'

She said, very deliberately, 'I've told you, I want to make a fresh start.' Her expression left him in no doubt that she was both serious and determined.

Simon was at a loss; he ran both hands through his grey curls in a gesture of puzzled surrender. 'When do you want to begin?'

'In the morning?'

On Thursday morning at five minutes to nine Simon went downstairs to unlock, almost willing to believe that the visit had been a dream. But Morwenna was waiting on the doorstep, trim and neat in a green mac, her hair tucked into a matching waterproof hat.

Simon fumbled with the lock, aware of Jeremy Scott watching from next door.

'I'm sorry; I didn't expect . . . I would have come down sooner . . .'

She came in, crisp and business-like. 'If you will show me where to put my things . . .' Then seeing his blank confusion, 'Never mind, I'll find somewhere.'

They were halfway down the shop. 'Don't forget your mail.'

He went back to collect it from the wire basket.

She wanted to know at once the kind of work she would be doing and he spent an hour explaining the records he kept and his system of accounts.

'You've no stock control? I mean you don't keep a running account of sales against purchases?'

'I'm afraid not.'

'It's quite simple with a small computer and among other things it helps to keep a check on theft.'

Already Simon felt that he was being managed.

As ten-fifteen approached he was on tenterhooks deciding whether to face the market routine or put off the inevitable to another day.

'At about this time I usually meet two or three friends in the market for coffee. I close the shop for a quarter of an hour. I don't suppose you would like to join us?' He prayed that she would refuse, while trying to imagine the situation if she did not.

'No, but don't bother to close; I shall be all right.' She added, 'I forgot to say that I'm away at weekends – Saturday lunchtime until Monday morning.'

'That's no problem.'

In a daze he arrived in the market where the others were already briefed and waiting. The fat woman served him with his coffee and chocolate biscuit, when Jeremy Scott opened the bowling.

'Was that who I think it was on your doorstep this morning, Simon?'

He plunged. 'It was Morwenna Barker. She's come to work for me.'

Little Simms chuckled. 'You're a dark horse, Simon!'

Burrows, judicial as ever, came in last. 'Was it your idea?'

'No. She turned up yesterday afternoon and asked for the job. What could I do?'

Burrows nodded. 'I see that, but you should ask yourself what she's up to. The Barkers never do anything without a reason and in this case it can't be money, not on what you'll pay her.' A pause for consideration, then the diagnosis. 'If you ask me, there's more in this than meets the eye.'

Simon did not need to be told that a large stone had been dropped into his small pond.

On a day of misty rain and blustery winds Detective Superintendent Charles Wycliffe, after an absence of many weeks, called at his favourite bookshop. The sign above the bulging Dickensian window of small panes read, 'Simon Meagor, Antiquarian Bookseller'.

Wycliffe pushed open the door, listened with satisfaction to the familiar 'ping' of the little bell, and found himself in the cave-like shop where several banks of head-high bookshelves were dimly lit by dusty bulbs on dangling flexes.

He recaptured the delectable, faintly musty smell of the place and started to walk down the nearest aisle. Almost at once he met Simon Meagor coming to meet him.

'Ah, Mr Wycliffe! How nice to see you. It must be several weeks.'

Wycliffe said, 'It was just after Christmas when I was last in Falmouth. I don't suppose you have anything for me?'

'I really think I might have. Last time you were here you will remember that we talked about Thomas Creevey. Well, I've got his papers in the Maxwell edition of nineteen hundred and three . . .'

Simon shared with his customer an enthusiasm for biographies, letters and journals, but there was something more; he sensed an affinity with the man, a common difficulty in aligning himself with the grain of life. It was a problem of integration. Simon suspected that for Wycliffe too, top policeman though he was, the recorded fragments of other lives might offer both reassurance and a yardstick.

The difference was that for a man like Wycliffe there could surely be no dark shadow reaching out from the past.

As usual Wycliffe walked towards the office space at the back of the shop and Simon followed.

To Wycliffe's surprise there was a girl seated at Simon's desk. She was making entries in a loose-leaf ledger and a shaft of grey light from the rain-streaked window shone on a cascade of red hair, all but hiding her face.

In the months ahead Wycliffe would recall that scene, which had the quality of a pre-Raphaelite painting.

For some reason Meagor seemed sheepish. 'This is Morwenna, Mr Wycliffe. She's helping me in the business.' He turned to the girl. 'Morwenna, this is Mr Wycliffe, one of our most valued customers.'

The girl looked up and Wycliffe received a momentary glance from the blue eyes before she returned to her work. Had her lips moved in a murmured greeting?

Strangely uneasy, Meagor said, 'I'll get the Creevey.'

Wycliffe left with his book. As he walked along narrow Moor Street towards the Strand he wondered. What was so remarkable in the fact that Meagor had acquired an assistant?

That evening, back home, he told his wife Helen of his visit to the bookshop. 'I happened to be in Falmouth, so I looked in.'

Helen too nurtured certain enthusiasms; gardening and botanical art, with a top dressing of music, and Simon supplied her with early gardening books, herbals and botanical prints, which she treasured.

'Simon's got himself an assistant, a beautiful young redhead. It seemed a bit odd somehow.'

Helen looked up from her newspaper. 'Why odd? If you think Simon might have designs on the girl, I'm sure you're way out. If anything he's more likely to be gay.'

To his surprise Simon soon came to accept Morwenna's presence in the shop. She had very little impact on the basic routine of his days and he had to admit that in no time at all she had got to grips with the nature of the business and with the paperwork. He was getting used to seeing her at her desk and he was more than content to leave her in charge while he took time off for things that would otherwise have meant closing the shop.

'I'm going out, Morwenna. I shan't be long.'

The past was never mentioned between them.

But he was not looking forward to the time when either of his children, Rebecca in particular, would decide to drop in.

She arrived one afternoon when the sun was shining and the aisles between the bookshelves were shafts of dusty light. As usual he came upon her unexpectedly browsing among the books.

'Becky!'

Like her mother, Becky was tall, fair and slim, and possessed of a facility to appear, rather than to approach. There was an impression of vagueness, of insubstantiality, entirely deceptive when it came to the nitty-gritty of life.

'How's your mother?'

'She's all right. I suppose you know she's senior partner now that old Grylls has packed it in. She's working all hours.'

Judith was a solicitor.

'And you? Great plans, I suppose, now you've got your finals?'

'I've got to get experience. I'd just as soon it wasn't with Mother's firm but that's what she wanted and Mother gets her way.' She broke off. 'Do you mind if I borrow this?' It was Simone de Beauvoir's *The Second Sex*. 'I won't keep it long. I've brought back the Virginia Woolf thing.'

Becky rarely left without a borrowed book, usually a biography, and Simon saw this as a bond between them.

So far they were only halfway down the shop and Simon was hoping to stop her there, but in vain.

'Oh!'

Morwenna was sitting at her desk, typing. She looked up, but carried on with her work. Before Simon could speak Rebecca had moved away up the aisle. The chill was perceptible.

At the shop door Simon said his piece. 'Morwenna has made a lot of difference to me. I'm not so tied and she's so good with the paperwork.'

'Isn't she the daughter of the man who . . .'

'Yes.'

A look which reminded him of his wife. 'I hope you know what you're doing, Dad.'

He watched her as she walked away, and until she

turned the corner into the Strand. That self-possessed young woman, warning him, was his daughter.

Incredible! He was troubled.

Another rainy Monday morning, two months after Morwenna started work in the shop. She arrived as usual at a few minutes before nine. They rarely greeted each other.

Morwenna hung up her raincoat and hat, ran a hand round the back of her neck, lifting her hair and letting it fall into place. She sat at her desk, then said casually, 'I shall have to look for new lodgings. The Burtons need my room.' She added, 'I've got a week.'

Although little was said, as the week went by he felt under a growing compulsion to offer her one of the spare rooms in the flat and on the Friday morning, feeling as though the words were being forced from him, he said, 'I suppose you could have one of the rooms upstairs until you find somewhere that suits you.'

She responded as though the offer was already taken for granted. 'What about the rent?'

He was embarrassed. 'I don't want any rent.'

She was removing the cover from her typewriter and no more was said. But that evening she moved in.

'This room was Becky's. She was only twelve when she left with her mother. Make any changes you like. In any case, I don't expect you'll want to keep the pin-ups.' It was Simon's joke, but she did not smile.

'Anyway I hope it will suit you.'

Simon was behaving as though she would be doing him a favour by agreeing to take the room, but he had serious misgivings. For ten years he had lived entirely alone; no female company, and looking for none. Now he had been induced to share his flat with a young woman – and this particular young woman.

But as time went by he became accustomed to flimsy items of underwear in the bathroom, to the prevalence of her favourite perfume, to glimpses of her flitting between bathroom and bedroom, naked except for a towel held to her breasts.

Once or twice he wondered vaguely what might happen if he followed her; and one morning he did, standing at the open door of her room. Was it possible that she was being provocative? She had stepped into her knickers and was pulling them up over her thighs. She looked at him with neither annoyance nor anticipation, but with indifference. 'Did you want something?'

It was a long while since he had been so close to a naked woman and this woman was beautiful and, he supposed, alluring, but he felt nothing; no excitement, no desire.

It was about now that he began to realize the extent to which his peace of mind, even his self-confidence, was being subtly undermined. It was not that she spent that much time in the flat. In the evenings she went out for her meal and she was often out for the whole evening. Even when she was at home she kept to her room, and every weekend she was away from Saturday lunchtime until Monday morning.

But there had been a change in the atmosphere and in her attitude towards him. He could not find words for it. Certainly there was a coolness which seemed deliberate, but there was much more to it than that.

Lunchtimes were difficult. His snack lunches at the

pub across the way were no more. For no reason that he could discover Morwenna had acquired a microwave oven, and lunch consisted of quick-fix meals from Marks and Spencer.

Sitting opposite each other at the kitchen table they would eat for the most part in silence. From time to time he would look up from his plate and catch her watching him, her eyes coldly appraising.

At first he had tried to start some sort of conversation. 'On the radio this morning they were saying . . .'

But she would look at him, her expression blank, and his voice would falter and fade away. At the appropriate time she would say, 'Do you want anything more? If not, I'll make the coffee.'

A little later it would be his turn. 'I'll feed Lady Lu and then I'll go down to the shop . . . I've one or two things to do before we open.'

Why had she come? Why had she forced herself on him? Was it only to achieve this?

It was the last day of July in the middle of a heatwave. The town was teeming with summer visitors; cars and pedestrians vied with each other in the narrow main street, catching tantalizing glimpses of the harbour through opes and alleys. At the entrance to the little pier and on the quay boatmen offered trips to all the exotic-sounding places that fringed the harbour, estuary, creeks and bay.

All this went on within a couple of hundred yards of Simon's shop, but Moor Street with its market was a separate world.

Simon was concerned. Morwenna had gone off for the weekend as usual and so far, after each weekend away, she had arrived back well before nine; now it was past ten and she had not returned.

As with any disturbance to his routine he was on tenterhooks. He stayed at the office end of the shop where he could see the yard, watching for her little yellow Mini.

Then the telephone rang.

Morwenna's voice. 'Yes, it's me. I am not able to come back at the moment . . . It may be a couple of days; I can't say exactly. You can take it out of my holidays if I'm due for any.'

'Are you all right? Can I get in touch with you?'

But there was no response; Morwenna had cut him off.

He dialled 1471 but the disembodied voice informed him that the number had been withheld.

Simon was puzzled and a little annoyed. But looked at objectively, Morwenna had led a life altogether apart from the shop about which he could only guess. Was it surprising if there was the occasional crisis? The best thing was to carry on as usual.

And very soon he began to feel oddly cheerful; it was like an unexpected holiday.

At ten-thirty Simon went to join the others in the market café, a routine never seriously interrupted, but he had to resort to his 'Back in fifteen minutes' card and lock the shop door.

Since the original confrontation his problem had not been mentioned again. Now he had to decide whether or not to say anything about Morwenna. They would find out soon enough if he didn't.

'Morwenna's gone away for a few days.' A weak smile. 'So I'm on my own.'

Burrows looked both knowing and patronizing. 'Good for you, boy! You've come to your senses. There's been talk, but it'll soon die down if you give it a chance. Where's she gone?'

Simon hesitated. 'St Ives, I think.' And he added after a pause, 'Staying with her aunt.'

He realized as soon as the words were out of his mouth that he had blundered.

Burrows leered. 'That's all right then; as long as it's not some discreet little clinic.'

For once Simon lost his temper. 'Don't be so bloody insulting!' Then, embarrassed, he looked at his watch and muttered, 'I've got a customer.' He got up, leaving half his coffee and the whole of his chocolate biscuit.

Burrows called after him, 'It was only a joke!'

As Simon let himself into the shop the telephone was ringing. Morwenna? No. A man's voice. Nicky Barker. 'I would like to speak to Morwenna.'

'She's not here.'

An edge of impatience. 'When will she be there?'

Simon floundered. 'I don't know . . . She's gone away.'

'Gone away? Where?'

Simon felt that he was being persecuted, and at a total loss he replaced the telephone.

Another mistake.

He was beginning to realize how embarrassing it would be if Morwenna was away for long without him knowing where she was. Surely she would phone again? . . .

But by Thursday Morwenna had still not returned and there had been no further message. Now, despite his concern, he found himself drifting back into his old routine. At one o'clock he crossed the road to the pub where, pre-microwave, he had been a regular customer for their snack lunches.

The waitress, a woman of about his own age, greeted him like an old friend. 'Good to see you again, Mr Meagor! Morwenna not back yet? . . . I suppose it's a lager to start – the usual half of Stella? . . . Then there's baked potato with ham – and that used to be one of your favourites. Served with a nice bit of butter.'

As she was leaving with his order she turned back and whispered, 'Don't take any notice of what they're saying about you, it's wicked!'

There were several occupied tables in the L-shaped space in front of the bar and as in most pubs the lighting was dimly sinister so that it was a minute or two before he spotted Nicky, Morwenna's cousin. It was odd; he seemed to be looking straight at Simon but there was no hint of recognition and Simon felt uncomfortable, threatened.

He ate his baked potato without enjoyment and left before the waitress brought his usual coffee.

By a quarter-past two when he reopened the shop he was beginning to recover his poise. Twice since his original visit Nicky had come to see him and Simon had given him money. If he came this afternoon should he pluck up courage and go to the police?

As it happened the afternoon was unusually busy with visitors actually buying books and he had no time to return to the parcel which had arrived that morning. He felt that he was getting back into the rhythm of his days. Then at four o'clock the telephone rang.

'I want to speak to Morwenna.'

He played for time. 'That's Nicky, isn't it?'

'What's that to do with you? I want to speak to Morwenna. Is she back?'

'No.'

'And you still don't know where she is?'

'No.'

'When did you say you expected her?'

'She said a couple of days but . . .'

'But what?'

Simon waffled. 'She didn't want to tell me where she was and I had the impression that she was trying to put me off; that she might be away longer.'

Nicky was unimpressed. 'That's all my arse. I want to know what's happening to my cousin, and I want to know pretty damn quick or you might find yourself running into a spot of bother.'

The line went dead.

Another threat. He was becoming entangled in a situation which was inexplicable and alarming. One thing was clear; he would have to do something more than sit back and wait. The police? Yes, but he couldn't face it at this stage.

He decided that he must pluck up courage and phone Morwenna's aunt at St Ives. What was she called? . . . Rowe – that was it. Morwenna's mother was a Rowe. He narrowed down three pages of Rowes in the phone book to a dozen entries for St Ives and finally to one that seemed promising: M. Rowe, Ardevera House, the Warren. Morwenna had some-times spoken of her Aunt Molly.

He was absurdly nervous.

'Miss Rowe? . . . Miss Molly Rowe?'

'Speaking. Who is it?' The voice was a refined croak, the manner peremptory.

Simon introduced himself. 'I'm anxious to get in touch with Morwenna. I haven't seen her since Saturday. She telephoned me on Monday but didn't tell me where she was and I wondered if she might be with you?'

'No, she is not with me. If she didn't tell you where she was she obviously didn't want you to know. She's been living with you, hasn't she?'

'No . . . I mean she has a room in the flat above the shop but—'

'Never mind the buts; perhaps she's come to her senses. Has she taken her car?'

'Yes.'

A momentary hesitation, then, 'I'm quite sure she knows what she is about.'

Simon felt battered. He was beginning to realize how little he knew about Morwenna. It was six years since her father's trial and in that time she and her mother had moved away from the town, her father had committed suicide after being released from prison and her mother had died. Through all that she had grown from a schoolgirl to a young woman; she had acquired a business training and held down a job, but he did not even know where or how she had been employed.

'I shall have to do something.'

At closing time that evening there was a summer storm with a torrent of rain. Water chuckled in the downpipes and dribbled from a cracked gutter over the market entrance. It was almost dark at six o'clock. Thunder rolled in the distance and cracked overhead.

With each lightning flash the lights dimmed. The flat seemed gloomy, chilly and damp.

Feeling guilty, as though about to commit some disreputable act, Simon went into Morwenna's room and shut the door behind him. It was the first time he had seen the inside of her room since she moved in.

Judith had taken scarcely anything with her of the marital home and Morwenna had made few changes in this room that had been Becky's. It was a plain bedsitter, lacking only the youthful imprint Becky had left upon it with her posters and cut-outs Blu-Tacked to the walls.

It looked now as though the occupant might return at any moment. The bed was made up, the wardrobe door was open and clothes were hanging inside. Among the toiletries on the table there was a comb with wisps of red hair glistening in the light.

Up to a point he was reassured; she meant to come back, otherwise she would not have left so much that was hers behind; intimate things such as clothes and toilet gear, and a framed photograph which she kept on the dressing table. It was a head-and-shoulders studio portrait of her mother to whom she bore a striking resemblance.

But it was no less urgent to get in touch with her and there must be papers, letters, something in this room that would help him. He tried the single drawer of the dressing table and then turned without much hope to the wardrobe. He was immediately confronted by three handbags on a shelf. Two were limp and empty – dress bags for special occasions – the third was the usual piece of light luggage that is every woman's standby. He knew that bag – he ought to, she was rarely parted from it.

Simon spread its contents on the bed: compact and lipstick, a comb, a few tissues, a ball-point, a slim purse containing several notes and some coins, a cheque book, credit cards, driving licence . . . There was also a letter written in a girlish hand. It seemed to be from someone she had worked with.

He scanned pages of innocuous chit-chat as the writing deteriorated into a scrawl, but on the final page he was brought up with a jolt. He read over the ragged lines three times before he fully grasped the implication of what had been written. The telephone was ringing on the landing but he could stand no more.

Near panic, Simon put his hands over his ears in an attempt to cut out the sound until the ringing stopped.

For a while he paced around, in and out of the rooms, up and down the passage. This place which had been his home for most of his adult life was suddenly hostile. It was as though he were living through a bad dream, in which everything that was familiar and agreeable had been subtly distorted and made repellent.

He went into the kitchen where in one of the cupboards he kept a bottle of sherry. Amontillado. He filled a tumbler to about one-third and drank it off. The sweet, slightly syrupy liquid warmed his inside and he felt better. But he realized that for once what he needed more was company; people about him.

It was only a step across the street to the pub and though it was still raining he did not bother with a raincoat or hat. He pushed open the familiar swing doors and entered the bar.

Several men were drinking, standing round the bar, and among them was Nicky Barker. He had not noticed before that Nicky's jet black hair was drawn into a pony tail at the back. Nicky was carrying on an animated conversation with his neighbours, and while Simon stood watching there was a burst of laughter.

Simon retreated and stood for a while in the shelter of the canopied entrance. The rain was unrelenting.

Suddenly everything seemed to become clear; he thought he understood; he was the target of a conspiracy, a conspiracy to demoralize, perhaps to destroy him. It all seemed to fit: Morwenna's disappearance, the telephone calls, the way in which he seemed to be haunted by Nicky – yes, and the letter; above all the letter which had been left for him to find and read.

Then he began to have doubts; it seemed so incredible. Was he becoming paranoid? And the sherry was beginning to affect him. He looked up at his flat where the light was still on in his attic room, but the thought of returning there alone was insupportable. The Queen's was just around the corner in the High Street . . .

The Queen's – yes. And why not?

He set out, almost running, keeping close to the house. Once his foot slipped off the kerb into the streaming gutter.

The Queen's had known better days and still retained something of its former distinction. When Simon blundered into the lounge bar his hair was plastered to his head, his jacket was wet through, his trousers clung to his legs and one shoe squelched as he walked. Drinkers at the tables paused in their talk to take stock of the phenomenon. Eddie Burrows was there; the moist eyes were looking straight at him and the thin lips were twisted in a sardonic grin.

For a moment Simon stood his ground, then, for the second time that evening, he turned tail and fled.

In the vestibule with its fake marble walls there were toilets. One door carried a white-enamelled plaque, 'Gentlemen'. Did it occur to him that he might lay the ghost?

At any rate he pushed open the door. Nothing had changed; the four massive stalls of glazed earthenware, lightly crazed; the sinks with their brass taps; the green and white tiles on the floor; and the three cubicles with their panelled doors and engaged/vacant discs.

Once more he saw Timmy Roach lying on the floor, his head in a pool of blood. Once more he saw the door closing behind someone leaving . . . How much of that person had he actually seen? Enough to identify him beyond any reasonable doubt?

That evening more than six years ago was the true beginning.

It was still short of nine o'clock and Simon, wearing his dressing gown, was drying his wet clothes in front of the gas fire in his little room. Lady Lu was curled up asleep on the hearthrug. Outside the storm had spent itself and there was an unnatural silence in which he could hear a continuous murmur of voices from the pub across the way. There were occasional shouts and guffaws and he felt sure that Nicky Barker was continuing to be the life and soul of the party.

His second visit to the Queen's in six years had laid no ghosts nor answered any questions.

At eleven o'clock, when the pub closed, he and Lady Lu were settling in bed. The late drinkers were leaving and he listened with something like envy to the cheery voices and the shouted 'goodnights'. Suddenly there was a crash of breaking glass followed by another. He padded downstairs in his bare feet and through to the front of the shop. The light from the street lamp showed him that two of the small panes of his shop window had been smashed. The street outside was quiet.

There was nothing he could do until morning. He went back to bed and lay awake, trying to decide what he must do then. The police. He must report Morwenna as missing.

The decision made, he fell into a fitful sleep.

Chapter Three

Detective Superintendent Wycliffe was sorting
through dead files which should have been returned to
Records weeks earlier. Diane, his personal assistant,
who never trusted him with any office routine, super-
vised.

'You haven't initialled the docket . . .'

An afternoon in early August, a slack time for CID.
A heatwave seemed to have rendered the opportunist
yobs torpid, and August was never a month for the
professionals. Wycliffe, hot, bored and irritable,
brooded on times past and tribulations to come.

A tap at the door: DI Kersey. Doug Kersey must
have aged with the rest of them though he seemed
much the same; perhaps not quite so overtly and
disturbingly vigorous; some corners rubbed off.

'Am I interrupting something?'

Wycliffe waved him to a seat.

Kersey laid several faxes on the desk. 'A report from
DI Lister, at Truro. And I've had a word with him on
the phone since.'

A *memento mori*. Through most of Wycliffe's time at
Area, Tom Reed had been synonymous with the
Truro sub-division. Now Tom had retired and DI

Lister had stepped into his shoes. Natural succession; but those words were beginning to have a hollow ring.

Kersey said, 'I think Lister has an attack of the jitters and wants his hand held. It seems a girl went missing about ten days ago. No obvious reason to flap at the time. She worked in a bookshop and shared the flat above the shop with her boss. She went off for the weekend as usual and hasn't been seen since. Nobody seems to know where she spent those weekends, which seems surprising.' Kersey stifled a yawn. 'Anyway, now—'

Wycliffe cut in, 'Where is this bookshop?'

'Falmouth.' He pulled a fax towards him. 'Chap called Meagor owns a shop; Simon Meagor. Bit of a weirdo according to Lister.'

Wycliffe saw in his mind's eye a tall, ungainly figure shuffling along one of the narrow alleys between his bookshelves, 'Ah, Mr Wycliffe! . . . I may have something for you.'

Kersey had not finished. 'Seems as though Meagor has been having a rough passage lately: menacing phone calls, a couple of bottles through his shop window, and a spray-can artist at work on his front wall. Not at all friendly.'

This time Kersey failed to control his yawn. 'Sorry! Late night. In effect they're accusing him of having done away with the girl. No real evidence, but who needs evidence when there's a sitting duck?'

It was on his last visit to the shop that Wycliffe had seen the girl. 'Morwenna helps me in the business . . .' Meagor, oddly self-conscious.

'Mr Wycliffe, one of our most valued customers.'

The girl had looked up, her blue eyes expressionless. Had her lips moved in acknowledgement before she returned to her work?

Wycliffe could recall the scene in vivid detail: the bleak, sparsely furnished office, the rain-streaked window and the girl's red hair shimmering in the grey light.

In the four or five years he had known Meagor he had pigeon-holed him as a loner, comfortably set in his mould and, like many of the breed, not at ease with women. It had been a surprise to find him with this girl assistant, and it was a greater one to learn that she had been sharing his flat.

Kersey looked at him in mild surprise. 'Are you still with me, sir?'

'Yes. Yes, of course! About the girl. You say she lived with Meagor in the flat over the shop?' Wycliffe was still coming to terms with this highly improbable scenario.

A Kersey grin. 'I don't know how far he was living with her but she certainly shared his flat. Anyway, Lister is under pressure. In addition to the mob reaction there's the girl's relatives. As I said, in effect, they're accusing the bookseller of doing away with her. And Meagor's own family isn't exactly rushing to his defence.'

'His own family?'

'He's married; separated from his wife. Two grown-up children, a boy in his late teens, a girl in her early twenties. The wife is a solicitor.'

Curiouser and curiouser! Wycliffe found it hard to believe that he was hearing about the same man; the reclusive bookseller, as much a part of the shop as the books he treasured and, sometimes with reluctance, sold.

'What do we know about the girl and her family?'

'She's called Barker, Morwenna Barker. Her father was a builder in a fair way of business. He had his yard in Falmouth but he and his family lived a few miles outside, near Constantine. Anyway he was sent down for manslaughter six years ago and at that time the girl and her mother went to live with an aunt in St Ives.'

Kersey, being Kerseyish, paused to savour his next morsel. 'There's a twist in the tale: Meagor was the principal witness for the prosecution.'

This was all too much for Wycliffe and he sidestepped. 'Is this man, Barker, still inside?'

'No. He was released on parole after serving about half his sentence and went to join his family in St Ives. Within a few weeks he topped himself; then, just over a year later, his wife died of a heart attack.'

Wycliffe's credulity was being stretched. 'And, after all that, the girl first went to work for Meagor and then shared his flat?'

'Odd, isn't it? I suppose it's not surprising that there's a fair amount of local feeling.'

'Apart from this aunt, does the girl have any other relatives?'

'A cousin, a toe-rag with a record, according to Lister; probably responsible for most of the aggro against the bookseller.'

'What is Lister doing about it?'

'What you'd expect. He's taken statements from the parties concerned and he's trying to find out where she spent her weekends. Apparently she was off somewhere every week from Saturday till Monday but nobody seems to know where.'

Kersey stroked the sparse bristles of a nascent beard. 'Of course Lister has checked on Meagor's movements, circulated the girl's description with a photograph, and the details of her car. He's appealed for help from the public and gone a bit over the top in setting up an incident van near the town centre. More for show, I think, than use. But, being Lister, he's got to be seen to be doing something. He says there's not much point in organizing a search until he's got some idea where to look. And that sounds reasonable.'

'Does he really think something's happened to the girl?'

A characteristic shrug. 'Lister is hedging his bets. He's worried that her body might turn up in a ditch somewhere while he's been sitting on his backside.'

'Tell him to keep us informed.'

Kersey said, 'He's only too anxious to do that already.'

Wycliffe was thinking of the bookseller. To him Meagor had been more than the man who happened to own his favourite bookshop. There had been in Wycliffe's attitude a trace of envy. Meagor had found a niche, mildly academic, into which he fitted like a rabbit in its burrow, safe as long as he didn't poke his head out too far. In day-dreams Wycliffe had played with the notion that in other circumstances it was the kind of life that could have been his. It was even possible that he might have become, indeed that he was, at heart, that kind of man.

Myths can be painful when they explode in your face.

He could have accepted the girl: Eve in the Garden. That would have been just credible. After all, Adam was innocent and gullible enough; the fig leaves came after the fall. But this particular girl . . . and the separated family . . .

Meagor had employed and shared his flat with the daughter of a man who in consequence of his testimony had gone to jail, and killed himself when he came out.

Wycliffe was surprised at the extent to which he had identified himself with the bookseller. If the investigation came to anything and he was involved, it would lead to some disturbing soul-searching.

A more or less public cock-up contrived by a young DC kept him late at the office, smoothing ruffled feathers and reasserting departmental discipline. In consequence he was late arriving home.

The sun had set and the estuary at flood tide was a silvery lake. The Watch House showed a single rectangle of yellow light which told him that Helen, a great conserver of everything, was in the kitchen.

She must have heard the car, for as he got out she was standing in the open doorway of the house. He was moved; that slim figure could have been Helen at any age, at any stage in their thirty-odd years of marriage, and as he joined her he kissed her with tenderness.

'What was that for?'

'Glad to be back.' It was true, but there was also a twinge of guilt that he had allowed himself to think of that other life which might have been his. That other self? He added, 'It seems a long time since I left home this morning.'

She squeezed his arm. 'Too long! Anyway, I've got a chicken casserole in the oven and a bottle of Chardonnay in the fridge.'

An hour later he was saying, 'The girl is twenty-three, her name is Morwenna . . .'

'You think it's possible that she's been murdered?'

'That's what some of the locals are saying and they're accusing Meagor.'

'Simon? It's just not possible! You don't suspect him, do you?'

Wycliffe told her, 'He's not the man we thought he was. That doesn't mean that he's guilty of anything but it puts him in a new light. If we need a suspect he's certainly eligible. For the past five months Morwenna has worked for him in the bookshop; for the past three, she's shared his flat. Whether she shared his bed is a question.'

'No! I can't believe it.'

'There's more; he's married but separated, and there are two grown-up children.'

Helen, duly astonished, stuck to her guns. 'Even so, I can't believe that he could murder anybody . . . He's such an unlikely man to be involved in any kind of violence.'

Yawning, Wycliffe said, 'I wish you or somebody would tell me how to pick the likely ones. Incidentally, I forgot to tell you, I have to go in tomorrow. The Chief has decided that Saturday morning is the best time for a meeting of departmental heads. Excommunication, the penalty for non-attendance.

'Anyway, I mustn't be late.'

★   ★   ★

By nine o'clock next morning Wycliffe was at head-quarters with his senior colleagues, waiting outside the padded door for Queenie, the Chief's grey-haired dragon, to summon them to the presence.

Bertram Oldroyd in his last year as chief showed no sign of letting go of the reins. They talked shop for fifty minutes on a tight agenda, then broke up. Management skills: that was the new name of the game and, in a country run by accountants, success-fully persuading people to commit *hara-kiri* on demand is at the core of management. Oldroyd was one of the old school but he recognized the inevitable.

When the meeting was over he asked Wycliffe to stay behind.

'Obviously, Charles, I don't know who the new boy will be but I've a pretty good idea. An organization man, a manager. Well-drafted memos will be the new currency. I pity the poor so-and-so really, pig in the middle between the Home Office, the CPS and the civil liberties lobby. It's a hot seat and getting hotter. You'll have to adapt.'

Wycliffe said nothing.

Oldroyd looked at his CID chief with a wry grin. 'I'm wasting my breath! You've always been one of the awkward squad, Charles, and a new backside in this chair won't change that.' A pause, then, 'It could have been you if you'd played your cards right a few years back but perhaps you had more sense. As it is, in your shoes, I'd get out while the going's good.'

'Thanks for the advice. I'll think about it.'

Oldroyd made a gesture of dismissal. 'Tell me when they find your redhead, Charles.'

For some reason Wycliffe was piqued. 'She's not *my* redhead! I saw the girl once, in the bookshop.'

Oldroyd grinned. 'I've no doubt you'll get to know her better, Charles.'

It was strange but from that time on the missing girl came to be known as 'Wycliffe's redhead'.

Wycliffe left the Chief's office feeling significantly older than when he went in.

Back in his own office he stood by the window, looking down on the continuous flow of traffic in and out of the city. A blowfly explored the desert of glass, creeping patiently up the pane to the top, then launching into frantic, buzzing flight and starting at the bottom again.

It was trying to get out. Or, as a biologist would say, it was exhibiting a positive phototaxic response, a response which would have taken it to freedom if some playful, perverted or indifferent god had not interposed a pane of glass.

Wycliffe was sympathetic.

Though his problem was of a different order and the capricious god was within him, the glass pane was real enough, and on the other side was a kind of freedom.

He opened the window and the fly, after a display of arrant stupidity, flew out.

He felt better.

Well, it was still Saturday and Helen was expecting him for lunch.

At the weekend most of the rooms in the building were empty and there was an unfamiliar echo on the stairs. On his way down he looked in on the CID duty room. DC Dixon was improving his mind with the *Daily Mirror* while DC Potter all but ruptured himself getting his feet off the desk.

'Very quiet, sir.'

'So it seems. Isn't DS Lane in this morning?'

'She was called down to the desk, sir.'

DS Lane, a parson's daughter, had worked with him on most of his important cases and she had resisted every attempt to push her up the ladder. There had been talk, but it had talked itself out. Now, at thirty-five, she seemed content with the very real authority she exercised through her boss.

He met her coming up the stairs. 'I'm glad I've caught you, sir. I thought you might have already gone. It's about the missing redhead, Morwenna Barker. It seems she used to work in the Camborne college library and there's a girl downstairs who worked with her. I'd like you to hear what she has to say.'

Wycliffe was introduced to a fluffy blonde, barely contained in a sleeveless top and stretch trousers. 'Tracey Bishop, sir.'

The girl seemed concerned and articulate.

'The first I heard that Morwenna had gone missing was this morning, when Mother pointed out a bit in today's paper. Morwenna and I worked together at Camborne before I got the job in the City library here, and was able to live at home.'

Tracey looked at Wycliffe, wondering whether this grave-faced man would understand. 'You know how it is; we kept in touch by a card at Christmas, and a letter, perhaps once in six months. Well, the last letter I had from her was about three weeks ago, and when I saw the bit in the paper this morning I thought I ought to show it to somebody.'

She held out three or four sheets of mauve note-paper covered on both sides with a girlish script. 'What matters is on the last page.'

Wycliffe read aloud:

' "I've kept what's worrying me until last. As you warned me, I made a big mistake in going to work for Meagor, and a bigger one in taking a room in his flat. I wanted to let bygones be bygones, but the man is a creep. I've got to lock myself in my room at night, and he's always around whenever I go to the bathroom or the loo. He's free with his hands even at mealtimes and when I'm working.

' "I would never have believed that anybody who looks as he does, and runs a respectable business, could behave like that. I shall have to leave, which is a pity, because the work suits me and, of course, I like working with books." '

Wycliffe finished reading. 'It's signed "Morwenna".' He turned to the girl. 'You will allow us to keep this for the time being?'

'You can have it. When she told me that she had gone to work for this man, and that she had a room in his flat, I just couldn't believe it! I mean, he was the one who got her poor father sent to prison and destroyed her family . . . It didn't make sense!'

A brief pause to recover her breath. 'I mean, you can't trust men anyway when they reach a certain age and begin to think they've missed something. But a man like him!'

She broke off, wondering whether this middle-aged policeman might have taken offence at this assessment, but she went on, 'Of course I wrote back, telling her to get out while the going was good. Now, I suppose, it's too late. I mean, I can't think what possessed her to go there in the first place. It's not as though she needed the money. Wenna owns property. She's very well off.'

Wycliffe said, 'We must thank you for coming in. Probably we shall need to contact you again, so perhaps you will leave your name and address with DS Lane . . . Oh, and by the way, where was Morwenna living when she worked with you in the library? Was she still with her aunt in St Ives?'

'No, she had a room in what was really a students hostel, just outside Camborne – Roskilly House it was called.'

When Lucy had seen the girl off she was surprised to find Wycliffe still standing, hands in pockets, silent and preoccupied. 'You seem shaken, sir.'

'I am. Gossip is one thing; this is more like circumstantial evidence.'

Lucy looked at him with concern. 'Is Meagor really a friend of yours?' Only Lucy would have dared put such a question.

Wycliffe bristled, then thought better of it. 'I suppose you could say that.' And a moment or two later. 'Anyway, I'm going down to talk to him, and I want you to drive me. That pair upstairs can look after the shop.'

'You're moving in over DI Lister's head?'

'I think you mean behind his back. No. You can ring him up and tell him, very nicely, that we're coming down. He can meet us at the incident van if he wants to. I must telephone Helen.'

*　　*　　*

At one o'clock Wycliffe, in his own car driven by Lucy Lane, was crossing the Tamar, a river with at least as much significance for the Cornish as the Channel once had for the English. The sun shone; it was hot.

Wycliffe experienced tremors of guilt. It was on the early side for meddling by a senior officer, but he needed to know what had gone wrong for Simon Meagor.

Lucy drove well and they made good time. In just over an hour they were away from the spine road and on the Falmouth side of Truro. A little later they parked by the incident van on the Moor, a large open space near the town centre, laid out as a car-park and bus stop. Lister was waiting for them.

'Sir! Glad you could come.' Which was unlikely, especially on a Saturday morning.

'You've met DS Lane?'

In the larger of the van's cubicles the three of them sat down. Lister drew Wycliffe's attention to the case file, waiting on the table like a holy book.

'Later perhaps.'

Wycliffe found difficulty in seeing Lister as a policeman. From his trendy haircut to his white shirt and dark suit, not forgetting a tie that was nicely balanced between the sombre and the flashy, Nigel Lister was a type specimen of the late-nineties young executive. He would have looked at home among upwardly mobile middle management anywhere – anywhere but a police station.

And it all went with a Tony Blair face of disarming innocence. But Lister was not much over thirty, and nobody would have been foolish enough to suppose that it was innocence which had taken him thus far up the greasy pole.

Wycliffe thought, Chief at forty-five?

Lister read Morwenna's letter and passed it back. 'It looks like first-hand confirmation of what's being said about the man.'

Wycliffe said that he wanted to try to reconcile all this with what he already knew of the bookseller.

Lister was nettled. 'I had no idea that you knew the man, sir.'

'I buy books from him.' Wycliffe closed that line with finality.

Lister became cautious. 'No doubt a lot of the aggro is being stirred up by Nicky Barker – the girl's cousin. He's a layabout with a string of drug-related convictions. But this letter gives it substance and makes it much more likely that Meagor is involved in whatever has happened to the girl.'

From where he was sitting Wycliffe could see the entrance to Moor Street; the bookshop itself was just hidden by a curve in the street.

'I take your point, but while I'm here I would like a word with Meagor if you've no objection.'

Lister looked as though he might have. 'He's already made a statement.'

'Don't worry. I shan't tread on any toes if I can help it.'

Wycliffe and Lucy Lane left the incident van and walked to Moor Street. Buses and taxis pursued complex paths to their appointed waiting places. Other vehicles circumvented the mêlée, while pedestrians with all the ingenuity and courage they could muster dodged between. The sun still shone and it was hotter.

The bookshop was as he remembered it except that two of the window panes had been replaced by plywood, and part of the wall had been worked over by a spray-can artist with words like 'Lecher' and 'Pervert'.

Lucy said, 'Precise, if less colourful than most.'

A little fat man wearing a dirty cardigan and baggy trousers stood in the doorway of the china shop. 'You from the police? He closes Saturday afternoons, but he's in there.'

The closed notice was displayed behind the glass. Wycliffe tapped on the door and a moment or two later Meagor emerged from one of the aisles looking grey, sombre and very tired. He unlocked and opened the door.

'Ah, Mr Wycliffe.' The usual greeting, but wholly lacking in enthusiasm.

Inside, the same church-like stillness. Only Meagor had changed. They followed him down one of the aisles to his office at the back. A window opened on to a yard and the blank wall of the market house.

Feeling slightly foolish, Wycliffe said, 'This is Detective Sergeant Lane.'

He was looking around at everything as though to reassure himself that here too, nothing had changed. By chance the loose-leaf ledger on which the redhead had been working during his last visit was open on the table.

Meagor said, 'I don't know what I can say, Mr Wycliffe, other than what I've told the inspector.'

Wycliffe brushed this aside. 'I'll be blunt. I'm here

to try to sort out exactly what has happened, and to discover how far you are involved. I want to do this as painlessly as possible but you must co-operate.'

He added, 'Perhaps we could sit down.'

Meagor, flustered, went to fetch another chair, and they sat, Meagor on one side of the table, the police couple on the other.

Wycliffe said, 'I don't need to remind you of the gossip about you and your relations with the missing girl; you have evidence enough of the ill-will which has been stirred up. But this morning we received information which seems to support these allegations.' Wycliffe told of the girl who had visited police headquarters and handed over the last sheet of Morwenna's letter, now transformed by a polythene envelope into an exhibit.

Meagor took it clumsily and his hand trembled so that he had to spread the sheet on the desk top. At last he looked up, his features strained, fumbling for words, 'I don't . . . I can't . . . I mean, there is not a word of truth in this. Not a word! I've never at any time . . .'

'You agree that Morwenna wrote that letter?'

'Well, yes. I mean it's her writing, but there's not a word of truth in it. You have to believe me.'

From where he sat Meagor could look down the whole length of his shop to the front window. Wycliffe could imagine his feelings; that sense of being cut off, isolated by these intruders from the world that was his. And how long would it be before he could feel once more in possession?

Wycliffe relaxed the tension. 'None of this amounts to proof of anything at all but, coupled with

Morwenna's disappearance, you must realize that there are grounds for an investigation.'

Was Lucy thinking that he was going soft on a friend? At any rate she intervened. 'This girl came here and asked you to employ her?'

'Yes. I had a card in my window advertising for an assistant and one afternoon she simply walked in and asked for the job. She said she wanted to let bygones be bygones. I couldn't understand it; I was worried; but in the circumstances I could hardly refuse.'

'Did she suggest moving into your flat?'

'Not then. That came later. She had been here about two months and everything was going smoothly. She was very good in the business and the past was never mentioned. She was lodging with people in a house on the Bar, then one day she said they wanted her room and she was having difficulty in finding another place.'

Meagor sighed, running a nervous hand through his grey curls. 'She put me in a position where I had to offer her one of the rooms in the flat. Just until she found somewhere.'

Wycliffe decided that it was his turn. 'Did things change after she moved in?'

A quick look. 'Oh yes. They did. It was hardly noticeable at first but gradually the relationship became strained. I mean, she did her work but she cut herself off more and more. There was hardly any conversation between us that was not directly concerned with the business. It became very uncomfortable.'

Meagor sat back in his chair. 'And then the gossip started.'

'So you blame Morwenna for the harassment you have suffered.'

Meagor ran his palm over the smooth surface of the desk top. 'I think she and her cousin Nicky must have contrived it. I think she came here to work and to live in order to put herself in a better position to undermine me.'

There was a reflective pause before he went on, 'I think she genuinely believes that it was my evidence at her father's trial which brought such tragedy to her family.'

'She could hardly blame you for witnessing to what you saw and heard.'

'I'm sure she had convinced herself that my evidence was false; at least questionable.'

'And was it?'

Meagor's hand fiddled nervously with the polythene envelope of Morwenna's letter. Finally, without looking up, he mumbled, 'If you had been in my position you would realize that it wasn't as simple as that.'

Wycliffe was icy. 'I shall study the reports of the trial and make sure that I understand the circumstances; then, perhaps, we shall return to the subject.'

Meagor looked abject but said nothing.

'All right, let's see if we can broaden the picture. I understand that Morwenna was away every weekend but you have no idea where she spent her time?'

'That is the truth.'

'You've checked with her relatives in St Ives?'

'As I told the inspector, I've spoken with her aunt but apart from saying that she didn't spend her weekends there she was not helpful.'

'What about evenings and her other free time?'

'She wasn't here much. She went out for her evening meal and she was often out for the whole evening. I've no idea where she spent her time.'

Wycliffe stood up and Simon thought that his immediate ordeal was over but Wycliffe said, 'While we are here I would like to see over the flat.'

'Morwenna's room – yes, of course. I'll show you.'

Lucy Lane was aware of the tension between the two men, neither of them knowing quite how to cope with their changed roles.

Wycliffe followed the bookseller up the stairs and Lucy Lane brought up the rear. On the landing they stopped. The door was open to the kitchen which seemed well equipped, but it was obvious that Meagor was no housekeeper and that Morwenna had not tried to be.

Meagor talked to cover his unease. 'Morwenna's room is on the right, down the corridor.'

The corridor was carpeted but crying out for a Hoover. Wycliffe saw the white-painted doors, each with its little china plaque.

A self-conscious laugh from Meagor. 'My wife put labels on all the doors so that we wouldn't lose our way. Morwenna had Becky's room – she hasn't changed it much.'

The single bed looked virginal; there was a white-painted dressing table, a matching mini-wardrobe and a few bookshelves over the bed. Well-to-do parents providing for the ephemeral needs of a young daughter.

Lucy asked, 'How old was Becky when you separated?'

'She was almost thirteen, and her brother, Jonathan,

was nine. Becky has passed her law exams and she's working in her mother's office to get experience.' A touch of pride.

'Your wife is a solicitor?'

'Yes. She has her own firm.'

Wycliffe saw what looked like the contents of a handbag, spread on the bed. 'What's all this?'

Meagor was embarrassed. 'I turned out Morwenna's handbag, trying to find some clue to where she might have gone.'

The bookshelves were well stocked with paperback novels and a few books of poetry.

Lucy looked in the wardrobe and glanced through the drawers; then she turned to Meagor. 'There's nothing to suggest that Morwenna expected to be away for any length of time.'

Meagor said nothing.

Wycliffe looked at him, a loner, in some respects a simpleton, caught up in a disturbing, perhaps a frightening, train of events. A victim? Possibly but was that the whole story?

'I want to see all the rooms if you have no objection.'

Meagor was uneasy, but he made no protest. They moved on. The living room and a double bedroom were both furnished to a standard recipe from an up-market store. Taste which offered nothing to offend and little to admire. Now in both rooms there was a prevailing musty smell of disuse and neglect.

In the bedroom Meagor said, 'We slept here before my wife left me.'

They had arrived at the end of the corridor and a flight of steep, narrow stairs led upwards.

'We haven't seen your room.'

With obvious reluctance Meagor said, 'I suppose you could say that the attic is my room. I like it up there.'

It was the room Wycliffe most wanted to see, and they climbed the stairs. A single bed covered with blankets that had probably never been washed; a table by the window, littered with papers; a kitchen chair and a leather armchair from which the stuffing was beginning to escape. A rough wooden shelf held a few books and a radio, and an old-fashioned gas fire stood against a small hearth with a cast iron mantelpiece.

A cat arrived from somewhere and, purring, began to rub around Meagor's legs.

Meagor looked at Wycliffe, apologetic and defensive. 'I've become accustomed to living alone and this is enough for me. I bring up books from downstairs as I need them.' He added after a pause, 'I go out for most meals.'

Wycliffe was silent. Neither Lucy Lane nor Meagor could have guessed at his thoughts. He was wondering, by no means for the first time, how he would behave if ever he was left entirely alone. Would he contract his world to a single room and live like a snail in its shell? It was not unthinkable.

He went to the window and looked out with approval. Below, the narrow street with its pub and shops; but beyond the rooftops there was a glimpse of the sea.

They went back, down the flight of narrow stairs, along the corridor and down to the back of the shop. At the bottom of the stairs they stopped by a cupboard with wired-glass doors. Afterwards Wycliffe wondered if it was by chance that they came to a halt there or whether Meagor had wanted to bring about what actually happened.

The contents of that cupboard were well known to Wycliffe; they were books which Meagor treasured as a collector and the two men had mulled over them more than once. Normally the doors were locked, but now they stood a little open and he could see gaps in the rows. He said, 'What's happened here?'

Meagor stammered, 'They're missing . . .' There was an awkward silence, then he went on, 'Hitchin's *History of Cornwall*, Gilbert's *Survey* in three volumes, Hooker's *Sikkim Rhododendrons*, Thomas Green's *Herbal*—'

Wycliffe cut short the list. 'What do you mean, *missing*?'

Meagor did not answer at once and when he did he lowered his voice almost as though he were saying something of which he was ashamed. 'Morwenna must have taken them with her.'

'Did she take anything else of yours?'

Meagor was becoming increasingly embarrassed. 'Some money. About three hundred pounds from the safe.'

Wycliffe was sharp. 'I've heard nothing of this. Did you tell the police?'

'It was only yesterday that I realized the books were gone. The same with the money. In any case, I shouldn't have done anything about it.'

'You realize this puts Morwenna's leaving in a very odd light? I mean, she takes your books and your money but leaves almost everything of her own behind. The one suggests that she had no intention of coming back, the other that she expected to return quite soon.'

Meagor shook his head. 'I can't understand it.'

Lucy tried. 'You said that you wouldn't have informed us about the missing books and the money; why not?'

A long pause, then, 'In view of everything . . . Her father . . .'

'Are you saying that you felt some responsibility for what happened to her father?'

'I think she held me responsible.'

Wycliffe was incredulous. 'And despite that she came to work with you and live in your flat.'

'I think she wanted to punish me. I can't think of any other explanation. But whatever you may think, Mr Wycliffe, I've done nothing to harm Morwenna.'

Wycliffe led the way back to the seats they had recently left. 'Just one or two more questions, Mr Meagor.'

Meagor sat, looking down at his hands, resigned.

'Do you have any relatives apart from your estranged wife and your children, Mr Meagor?'

The grey eyes became wary. 'A sister, Alice.' Then, realizing that more was required of him, 'She's married, and she and her husband farm Trecathyk, near Constantine. It was my home; where I was born and brought up. When father died he left the farm between the two of us but farming had no attraction for me.'

Another break, then, 'When Alice married, her husband bought me out. And so I came here. It was my chance to do what I most wanted.'

Wycliffe was looking at him with an odd expression.

At one level he was questioning a witness, a possible suspect, but at another he was adding detail to the picture he had of his bookseller.

'Do you see much of your sister?'

Meagor was sullen. 'I spend Sundays there.'

From where he was sitting Wycliffe could see into the yard. Meagor's discreet grey van was parked there. The yard was in shadow but the sun shone brilliantly on the blank red-brick wall of the market house.

'That is all for the moment, Mr Meagor. You will, of course, tell us if you have any news of Morwenna.'

On their way back to the incident van they dawdled in order to sort themselves out before rejoining Lister. Wycliffe admitted to being more confused than when he arrived.

Lucy asked, 'Are you thinking of getting a team together?'

He hesitated, 'What have we really got to justify it? Apart from gossip – gossip apparently inspired by the girl herself – there is nothing to implicate Meagor. The girl has gone missing for a fortnight; that's all we have.' And after a moment he added, 'But we can't just walk away.'

Lucy was silent and he turned to her. 'Any thoughts?'

'Look at it this way. If it's only our next step that you're concerned with, it seems reasonable to carry out a proper search of the premises where she was living.'

Wycliffe pondered. 'You're saying, turn Fox loose in the flat on a fishing expedition. All right, I'll go along with that.'

But he was still sufficiently identified with his bookseller to feel a twinge of guilt.

A hundred yards further on, he said, 'Another thing, Lucy, we must know more about Morwenna's father; about his trial and conviction. Get them to pull the file on the case and send it to HQ.'

Finally, as they were approaching the incident van, he asked, 'What did you make of Meagor as a man?'

It was Lucy's turn to hesitate, then she said, 'Weak, but dangerously honest.'

Wycliffe looked at her. 'You're a clever woman, Lucy.'

Chapter Four

When Wycliffe arrived home in the early evening the whole estuary seemed enveloped in stillness; the sky was blue, not a leaf stirred and even the starlings, regimented on the power line, were silent. Helen met him at the door.

'You look depressed.'

'Right first time, love.'

'There's somebody here to cheer you up.'

Their daughter Ruth. A big hug. The two had always been especially close, neither of them able to see wrong in the other.

After the break with her former boss and sleeping partner, Ruth now worked for a TV company, in personnel.

Sherry in the kitchen while Helen tried to prepare a meal.

Wycliffe looked at his daughter. 'How come?'

'Isn't it your birthday on Tuesday? Knowing you, you'll be working, so Mum and I thought we could celebrate by spending a quiet Sunday to-gether.'

At the back of his mind all day had been his chat with the Chief which, being translated, meant: 'Times are changing too fast for both of us. Do what I'm doing – get out while the going's good.'

In a nightmare scenario Wycliffe saw himself working for a still youthful Lister look-a-like with a degree in law and the mind of an accountant. The alternative, at the moment, seemed both logical and appealing.

That night Wycliffe and Helen lay awake for a while, reading in bed.

He said, 'Ruth seems happy and settled.'

'Yes.'

'You don't sound very sure.'

'Perhaps I'm afraid that she's closer to becoming a confirmed spinster.'

'As things are, she might do worse.'

Silence. He had said the wrong thing. Then, a page or two later: 'You've got to think of what life will be like for Ruth, Charles, when she's our age – with nobody.'

Sunday 13 August

The morning air seemed fresher, the sun was shining and on the Wycliffes' breakfast table there were three elegant packages waiting to be ceremonially unwrapped. They turned out to be: a monumental biography of Lytton Strachey from Helen, a notable addition to his Bloomsbury saga; a framed watercolour of the Watch House when it was still a coastguard property from Ruth; and a fantasic little Kikuyu cult-figure from son David in Kenya, which Helen must have held back for a day or two from the post.

Later there was a phone call from David, interspersed with contributions from their daughter-in-law and from Jonathan, aged six.

A very pleasant day: a walk along the shore to St Juliot, lunch in the pub and an afternoon spent working in the garden with Macavity the Second, the Wycliffes' cat. Like his predecessor, Macavity led a fantasy existence, chasing invisible mice, and making prodigious leaps into the air in vain attempts to catch a butterfly on the wing.

In philosophic mood, Wycliffe saw Macavity's antics as a parody of his own.

That evening Ruth cooked a meal to mark the occasion; a lazy spell sprawled on chairs in the garden followed.

'If I retired we could live like this.'

Helen squeezed his arm. 'And die of boredom?' But after a pause she added, 'I don't know. Perhaps not.'

Choices.

Monday 14 August

By eight-thirty on Monday morning Wycliffe was in his office. There was nothing to merit the early start. The slack time continued and so did the heat-wave. The truth was that he wanted to monitor the situation in Falmouth.

Diane arrived looking pristine. 'Good weekend?'

He was not in the mood. 'So-so. I was working all day on Saturday. Will you get Mr Kersey for me, please?'

On occasions like this, Helen would say, 'You can be a real misery sometimes, Charles.'

Kersey came in looking, as usual, like the morning after. He had a couple of files under his arm. 'Good morning, sir. Nice day.'

'Don't you start!'

Kersey grinned. They had known each other a long time. He unloaded the files on to Wycliffe's desk. 'The Barker case.'

Wycliffe glared at the kilo of paper and decided that it was not for him.

Kersey said, 'Don't worry; there's a précis. Somebody's boiled it down to an A4.' And he passed over the sheet.

Wycliffe read: ' "George Barker, builder, and Arthur Bunt, farmer, owned adjoining pieces of land near the village of Constantine, with outline planning permission for a housing development. Detailed planning was far advanced when they discovered that an access road, essential to the plan, was not a public highway but privately owned, and that it had been bought under their noses by a local wheeler dealer called Timothy Roach.

' "In his evidence Meagor told the Court that, after a dinner given by Falmouth and District Traders at the Queen's Hotel, he was in one of the cubicles of the Gents suffering from a severe gastric upset when he overheard a quarrel between Barker and Roach. There was the sound of a punch followed by a thud, and he came out to find Roach lying on the floor, his head in a pool of blood. It seemed that in falling Roach must have struck his head on a washbowl. Meagor had claimed that at that same moment he saw Barker leaving by the door into the hotel vestibule.

' "Barker's defence was a flat denial that he had been in the Gents at the relevant time.

' "This was countered by evidence from Arthur Bunt that Barker, in a very distressed state, had passed him in the vestibule only seconds before Meagor called for assistance." '

Wycliffe finished reading and pushed the paper across to Kersey. 'It puts us in the picture. Enough to be going on with.'

Kersey said, 'Do you think that's where it all started?'

Wycliffe's mind was busy with the scenes which must live in Meagor's memory of that evening. He said, 'I don't know what to think. We shall have to wait for some development. I've agreed with Lister that Fox will search the flat this evening – after the shop is closed. We've no justification for ploughing in much further on Lister's patch but make sure he keeps us informed.'

They were interrupted by a call from the switchboard.

'DI Lister, on the phone, sir. Says it's urgent.'

'Put him through.'

'There's just been a report from a chap in the Constantine area, sir. Dog-walking among the disused quarries he spotted a small yellow car, almost certainly a Mini, at the bottom of one of them. It's submerged in several feet of water. Pure chance that he saw it. This quarry is known locally as Job's Pit and I've got a map reference.'

Wycliffe, his emotions too deeply involved in the case, hardly knew whether to feel satisfaction in a possible breakthrough or misgivings about where it would lead. He told himself, not for the first time, that he was a bad policeman.

He collected his wits. 'Well, the first step is to get the underwater team out there. Will you see to that? If they identify the car as the girl's, then we must arrange for recovery. Keep in touch.'

It sounded confident and incisive – he hoped.

He passed the news to Kersey. 'So we're waiting on the frogmen.'

Kersey was untroubled by hang-ups. 'If it's her car and she's in it, at least we shall have something to work on.'

Lister excelled himself. By midday he was reporting that the car was Morwenna's, the registration checked, and an auburn-haired girl was in the driving seat.

Lister went on, 'It will take quite a while to get gear together, recover the vehicle and get her out . . . unless we can arrange a helicopter lift.'

Lister, a diplomat, floated the idea and let it go at that.

A helicopter lift meant the navy, and the navy meant money, but Lister was right.

Wycliffe spent some time briefing the Chief and convincing him, first that a helicopter was the only sensible answer, and second that the contingency fund, if there was still anything in it, should meet at least part of the cost.

Wycliffe wound up, 'One thing's certain, my budget won't stand it.'

Agreement of a sort was reached, and by half-past one he was persuading the navy to get busy. A helicopter, based at Culdrose Naval Air Station, would be available at 1500 hours and would need the following ground support . . .

Meanwhile Kersey was collaborating with Lister to raise a team and arrange transport. DS Fox, the squad's scenes of crime officer, was sent on in advance.

Canteen sandwiches for all concerned.

Wycliffe spoke on the telephone to Dr Franks, the pathologist. The two men had worked together for years and between them there was a relationship compounded of mutual respect, incredulity, irritation and affection.

'You want me there, Charles? Couldn't it be a suicide?'

'I'm not clairvoyant and I'm taking no chances. I'll give you the map reference. It's a bit off the beaten track and likely to be rough going in places so watch it if you're driving that lethal weapon you call a car.'

Shortly after two Wycliffe, with Lucy Lane driving, was on his way. Kersey had gone on ahead.

It was still hot. Wycliffe sat in front with the map on his knees. As they approached the area he gave regular instructions. 'We're just coming into Mabe Burnthouse, turn left down the hill in the village.'

As Lucy drove Wycliffe ticked off the evocative names; Mabe Burnthouse gave way to Antron and Argal, with its reservoir . . . 'Now we're joining a slightly mainer road; Lamanva, Treverva . . . We're getting warm.' The names rolled off his tongue like a litany. Wycliffe had become Cornish both by adoption and addiction.

Even the mainer road was getting narrower and

prone to frequent undulations. The dips were wooded with a splendid display of ferns in the hedges, while on the mounds trees were stunted and gnarled or non-existent. 'Here we are at Eathorne. Look out for some sort of lane on the right.'

As he spoke there was a great roar, and a helicopter passed low overhead so that they could hear the beat of the rotors.

Lucy said, 'Curtain up!'

At that moment they rounded a bend and came in sight of a lone policeman standing where a rough track led off into the wilderness. 'It's not far to where the vehicles are parked, sir, and that's quite close to the quarry.'

The stony track gave way to slippery, hummocky grass, and the whole thing was a miniature switchback. The view was non-existent, limited by low mounds and a cloudless blue sky. The hovering helicopter seemed very close.

Broken drystone walls defined ancient field patterns, antedating by centuries the devastation by the quarries. Then, abruptly, they came upon an area of open ground where police and other vehicles were parked, including a vehicle recovery truck and the mortuary van. At some distance a large cross, marked out in white tape, indicated where the helicopter would place its load. Men and women in and out of uniform waited in their vehicles with the doors wide to create a current of air.

Lucy parked in line and they got out. The sun beat down on the sparse soil and the heat was thrown back at them as they walked.

A gate in a crazy wooden fence was wedged open. It

carried a crude notice in faded red paint: 'Danger! No Access!'

The helicopter still hovered and expanding circles of sound raced across the countryside. They walked in that direction and almost immediately rounding a bluff, came upon the quarry. It had been gouged and blasted out of the hillside, leaving a sheer wall of granite more than a hundred feet high, but tapering away to nothing at the horns of the crescent and embracing a substantial lake. Vertical fracture lines in the face gave it the semblance of a massive architectural feature.

Now the surface of the lake was rippled by the blast from the helicopter overhead. The hoist had been lowered and two frogmen were attaching a sling which was presumably secured to the submerged vehicle.

The quarry faced north and the granite cliff cast a sombre shadow across the water so that, despite the sunshine and the blue sky overhead, it was an eerie place.

At the top of the cliff two tiny figures moved about with no apparent purpose against the sky. DS Fox, in charge of scenes-of-crime, would be one of them. Presumably it was from there that the car had plunged into the water. Fox would make sure that no stone remained unturned, no puddle or rut unexplored, and all would be embodied in a series of sketch-plans and photographs augmented by an ample text.

There was another group, near at hand, gathered at the margin of the pool, Kersey and Lister among them. Wycliffe, with Lucy Lane, joined them.

Greetings were exchanged by gesture as nobody

could hear themselves speak. In fact, the roar from the helicopter increased as the lift began.

The little yellow car broke surface and was soon clear. Water streamed back into the pool in a torrent.

The engine hood was gaping and the frame appeared to have been distorted, but the bodywork had held together. One of the front wheels was at an odd angle.

The helicopter gained height, manoeuvred briefly, then made off with its suspended load in the direction of the vehicle park.

Wycliffe said, 'Let's follow the navy.'

He was made uncomfortable by his new DI. Here, on the ground, on real business, Lister still looked as though he had just emerged from the proverbial bandbox.

The helicopter put down its load as though it were a basket of eggs, regained height, dipped in salute, and made off. The battered and mutilated Mini sat squarely on the taped cross.

A silver-grey Porsche erupted on to the scene, braked heavily, and skidded to a halt on the tinder-dry grass. Dr Franks, the rotund and ebullient little pathologist, had made his entrance.

'So what exactly is all this about, Charles?' The question was put at a distance of several yards as he advanced to join Wycliffe. 'I saw and heard the navy moving out.'

In temperament and outlook they were poles apart. At fifty-plus, a bachelor and a womanizer, Franks took a relaxed, pragmatic view of life, death, the universe and all that. A view which never failed to ruffle the susceptibilities of the Wycliffe psyche.

'So you've come.'

Before the mortuary men attempted the removal of the body from the wreck Wycliffe, Franks and Lister, with the police photographer, went over to see and to record what could be seen.

Franks loosened his shirt collar. 'God, this is worse than Marrakesh in July.' He liked to cultivate a weary globe-trotter image.

The windows of the Mini on both sides must have been already lowered when it plunged over the cliff and the windscreen though shattered had not splintered on impact with the water.

Morwenna's body was slumped forward in the driving seat as far as the constraining belt would allow. Her head rested on the steering wheel which was largely enveloped by her red hair.

The engine was switched off, the gear lever was in neutral and the hand brake off. Apart from the girl's body the car appeared to be empty; not a coat or mac, not even a handbag. The car doors had remained shut. Presumably if there was anything there it had been swept up in the rush of water; but the rush would have been inward, so was it likely that anything would have been swept *out* of the car? The frogmen were searching the lake bottom but from any point of view it was unlikely that they would be successful.

The police photographer recorded it all in a frenzy of clicking and whirring, two mechanics moved in to lever open the doors and cut through the belt, then at last the mortuary men were able to lift the body clear.

Morwenna was wearing a plain green top and matching trousers. As they placed her body on a ground sheet water dribbled away in rivulets.

The face had changed little from how it had been in life, and the hands were neither unduly pale nor swollen. It was still possible to look upon the body as Morwenna, the redhead of the bookshop. No foam at the mouth; no sign of the tongue protruding between the lips. She had not been long in the water and her death was not due to drowning.

But two or three hours in the open air and that same body would be no more than a counterfeit, the reality of death, divorced for ever from the recollection of a life.

He said, 'How long?'

The question was addressed to Franks but Lister, like a keen schoolboy anxious to make his mark, interposed, 'If it's any help, the temperature of the water at the level she was trapped is six or seven degrees Celsius. The quarry faces north so it's unlikely that the sun ever reaches the surface near the cliff. I'm told that the mineral content is likely to be high, so bacterial contamination is probably low.'

Franks looked at Wycliffe, grinning. 'Good, isn't he? If he goes on like this you won't need me. I'd say less than twenty-four hours in the water; and my guess is that she died shortly before immersion. I'll be in a better position to judge when I've had her on the table but if we don't get her out of this sun my job is going to be a hell of a lot more difficult.'

So Morwenna Barker, wrapped in a plastic body-bag, was carried in the blinding sunlight to the mortuary van.

The vehicle recovery truck moved into position and the wreckage of the Mini was lifted on to it and enveloped in plastic.

'To guard against possible contamination,' the expert explained.

Wycliffe, intrigued by the almost superstitious observance of ritual by experts, was moved to ask, 'Like getting wet?'

Standard procedures were set in train; the little car would be minutely examined by a mixed team of police vehicle examiners and specialists from Forensic. Accident investigators would inspect the ground leading to the quarry edge and report their interpretation of whatever signs remained.

Wycliffe spoke to Kersey. 'I want you to see that the coroner is notified and attend to the media. Lister will make arrangements for the coroner's officer. Take Lucy with you. She had better contact the girl's aunt in St Ives and, I suppose, Cousin Nicky. Lucy will have to arrange for the ID.'

Kersey said, 'A suspicious death – is that our line with the media?'

'No, simply that the cause of death is being investigated and, of course, the girl's identity has not yet been officially etablished.'

Wycliffe looked up at the quarry face. 'I'm going to take a look up there and have a word with Fox if he hasn't already left. I'll be at Lister's incident van inside the hour.'

There was no longer any sign of activity on the cliff top. Presumably Fox had finished and gone. So much the better. Wycliffe wanted to see for himself and he needed time to think. He glanced at his watch. Still only a little after five. The team was breaking up, moving out with their vehicles, and the quarry would soon be returned to its desolation. Obviously there must be a track by which vehicles could reach the cliff top, the route taken by Morwenna's car and by the SOCO truck. Fox, even with his slave-assistant, would not have manhandled his gear up that steep grassy slope around the perimeter of the quarry.

Wycliffe was about to drive off in search of this track when he changed his mind, got out, locked the car and started to climb.

A helpful copper, clearing up the last remnants of the circus, called, 'You can drive around, sir – by the road.'

'I know.'

Nobody, least of all Wycliffe himself, could have explained why he did this sort of thing. A self-inflicted penance? If so, what for? However, he reached the top, breathing hard, the knees of his trousers stained with green where he had slipped on the grass.

He stood for a while recovering.

The view was impressive. From the sea, glittering in the sunshine to his right, a great sweep embraced a significant area of mid and west Cornwall, but Wycliffe's interest was in the ground leading to the cliff edge. Fox would have it all neatly boxed in his camera, his charts and his notebook, and the accident investigator would visit the site, but Wycliffe needed to see for himself.

There was not that much to see. Quarrying seemed to have stopped roughly at the summit of the hill, and the ground was almost level for a few metres short of the edge. Wheel tracks were just visible in the sparse grass and at one point, about seven or eight metres from the edge, they were deeper, as though the little car had stopped there for some time.

Further still from the edge, as the ground sloped

away, the grass petered out in a hard, bare, stony surface where all trace of the wheels was lost. The track led downhill in a broad sweep to join the road perhaps a quarter of a mile away.

Wycliffe pottered around, trying to visualize what had happened. On the face of it there seemed to be a simple interpretation: the girl had driven to this spot with suicide in mind. She had cut the engine and stopped for a while, brooding on her decision and steeling herself to carry it out. Finally she had put the gear lever into neutral, released the handbrake, and started on the brief but terrible journey.

For an instant Wycliffe was in that little car as it reached the edge. He experienced that helpless emptiness as it tilted and plunged. The drop was at least a hundred and twenty feet and there would have been an interval of just over two seconds before the shattering impact. Then, a dramatic slowing of tempo as the water flooded in and the car sank.

But Morwenna had not drowned, so how and at what stage had she died? On the face of it this was a case of suicide. Had she died in the trauma of the descent?

It was only now that Wycliffe saw the possible significance of the fact that the ground was virtually level for some distance from the cliff edge. In fact there seemed to be a slight upward slope. With the gear lever in neutral and the engine switched off, it was unlikely that the Mini had been *driven* those last few metres. If not, from where had the impetus come to take it from rest and over the edge?

Had it been pushed? If so, the whole idea of suicide was put into question.

Wycliffe was shaken. Only the accident investigator would be in a position to give a worthwhile opinion about the angle and nature of the ground, and whether the Mini could have made it unaided over the edge.

Problems. But Wycliffe had seen what he had come to see, and he left, as the inestimable Poirot would have said, 'Given furiously to think'.

He made the descent inelegantly but there was no-one to see.

Chapter Five

Five-thirty that same afternoon, and Falmouth was winding down; shops closing, shoppers making for home. In Moor Street people were leaving the market with half-price, over-ripe fruit and ageing vegetables. For perhaps half an hour Simon had been standing just inside the open door of his shop, watching the goings and comings in the street. On the step Lady Lu, with the aid of teeth and tongue, performed an acrobatic and meticulous pedicure. He had not closed the shop but neither had he switched on any lights and the bookshelves stretched away behind him into cavernous gloom.

He had no reason for standing there other than a compulsive need to maintain some contact with the outside. Soon he would hear the sound of the iron grille being drawn across the market entrance and then it would remain closed until morning.

Because the doors were set at an angle to each other Simon could look into Jeremy Scott's shop across the narrow alley. He had watched Jerry sell an alleged Enoch Wood figure, a figure which had been in his window for years. Normally if he had spotted Simon he would have given a discreet

85

thumbs-up. But now the little man seemed careful not to see him.

Two days since Wycliffe's visit, and he had heard nothing; but he could find no consolation in that.

Strange. Events had transformed the man from a respected customer, almost a friend, into a threat. And yet, absurdly perhaps, he had the impression that Wycliffe was reaching out to him for a kind of reassurance. And failing to find it.

Of course it was absurd! He was vulnerable; trapped; with a compelling need to defend himself. But how? At bottom, perhaps, he was guilty.

Morwenna had come to work for him, and she had moved in to his flat. He had been made the subject of vaguely scandalous gossip which had developed first into a smear campaign, then into open hostility. When Morwenna had disappeared he had become the victim of telephone threats and vandalism.

If she really had set out to discredit him, to destroy his peace of mind, even to threaten his liberty, she had succeeded. He was being isolated. His son Jonathan no longer dropped in for those casual chats which kept them in touch. Becky still came to borrow a book or chat about her work, but now there was a reserve, a cautionary element in her attitude, as though she would say, 'Watch your step, Dad; you're in deep water.'

He closed the shop door, locked it and, followed by Lady Lu, went upstairs to his attic. He was in no mood for food. The clock on the mantelpiece showed three minutes to six but it was always slow. He switched on his radio for the local news and, as though by some stroke of fate, the first words he heard were:

'News is coming in of the recovery of a car, a yellow Mini, from the bottom of a flooded quarry near Constantine. Our correspondent understands that the car has been identified as belonging to Morwenna Barker, the young woman missing for more than two weeks from the bookshop where she lived and worked.

'Detective Inspector Kersey told us that the body of a young woman found in the car has not yet been formally identified and that it was not possible at present to say anything about how she died.

'Detective Kersey added that all the circumstances surrounding the discovery were already under investigation.

'Further details will be included in our later bulletins as they come in.'

So . . .

Simon stared at the radio in unbelief. That quarry; he had no doubt which it was – Job's Pit where, like all the children of the neighbourhood, he had played as a boy. As he turned away he had a disturbing image of Morwenna's red hair trailing in that dark, icy water.

He moved to his window and stood looking down into the street. It was so quiet that he could hear the conversations between passers-by.

A van was making its way along the narrow street – a police van, and it stopped just below him.

He was halfway down the stairs to the shop before there was a knocking on the shop door. He went to open it.

A very tall man stepped inside. A protuberant nose and receding chin gave him a beak-like profile. 'Mr Simon Meagor?'

Simon thought that he was about to be arrested but

the man held out his warrant card and went on, 'Detective Sergeant Fox. I have a warrant to search your flat.'

He felt bound to make some show of protest, 'But Mr Wycliffe . . .'

A thin smile on Fox's thin features. 'That wasn't a search, Mr Meagor; not by any means. Just a preliminary look round.'

They were joined in the shop doorway by a young black woman who had been driving the van. She introduced herself. 'DC Thorn.' In contrast with the sergeant her manner seemed friendly.

She turned to Fox, 'We'd better get this thing off the road, sarge, otherwise some rogue copper will do us for obstruction. Mr Meagor has a yard at the back; I'm sure he won't mind.'

When the van was parked Simon let the pair in by the back door.

'We'll start in the dead woman's room.'

The dead woman.

Simon said, 'I heard it on the radio . . .'

'Oh, yes?' And that was all.

Simon led the way upstairs, and on the landing the sergeant made a preliminary reconnaissance of the rooms, then, 'Perhaps you will stay in your living room for the present, Mr Meagor.'

But DC Thorn said, 'You're entitled to watch us if you want to.'

Lady Lu, unsettled, went to her bowl, sniffed the milk but did not drink. Meagor sat in one of the two armchairs at a loss what to do with himself . . . Every now and then there were noises from elsewhere in the flat as furniture was shifted about. He clenched his fists and thrust them deep into his trouser pockets. His home had been taken over; it was as though he no longer existed.

Perversely he was concerned at what seemed to be the irrelevance of their procedure. What did they expect to find? Was it merely a technique to harass him? Or was it part of a darker scenario that was taking shape in his mind?

Morwenna was dead. If he was arrested, if he was charged, would he have any coherent defence? If he was convicted . . . in his imagination there was a 'For Sale' notice outside his shop. In the flat, devoid of furniture, the tarnished paintwork and peeling wallpapers were open to inspection by anyone with an order to view. The shop was closed and his solicitor, who knew nothing about books and cared less, was arranging a sale which would be a field day for the cowboys in the trade.

The little world which he had largely created and grown into would vanish as though it had never been.

He could not have said how long it was before he was called from the passage by the man called Fox, 'Mr Meagor! Perhaps you will join me in your bedroom, please.'

As in a nightmare Simon followed him. The door to Morwenna's room was open and the young DC was going through the things he had left on the bed. With Fox leading he climbed the stairs to his attic. There the bed which normally blocked access to a wall cupboard had been pulled away and the cupboard door stood open. Inside was a single shelf on which several books were stacked.

Fox picked up a paper from the bed. 'Your list of missing books, Mr Meagor.'

He removed a book from the shelf. 'Hitchin's *History of Cornwall* . . .' He placed the book on the bed and reached for another, 'Gilbert's *Survey of Cornwall* in three volumes – one . . . two . . . three . . .'

The policeman behaved like a magician performing his star turn and Simon watched, transfixed.

When all the books had been transferred to the bed Fox reached into the cupboard once more and came out with a bulging envelope which he added to the books. 'Unless I am mistaken, here is your three hundred pounds.'

Simon found his voice. 'But it's not possible! I haven't been to that cupboard in years!'

Fox pointed to the floor space in the gap between the bed and the wall. 'Somebody has. This bed had been shifted quite recently before I moved it. The marks are clear in the dust.'

Simon stammered in his distress. 'But why? Why should I hide my own books? My own money? It makes no sense!'

'If you didn't hide them how could they have got here?'

Simon ran a hand through his hair. 'I don't know. Morwenna must have put them there. She must have!'

'Why would she do that?'

'I don't know. Unless she wanted to trap me or something. If I'd reported the books missing, and then they were found here . . .'

Fox smiled a thin smile. 'A bit elaborate, don't you think? Anyway, when could she have done it? It can't have been long before she left. Was she alone in the place for any length of time?'

Simon considered. 'No, not really.' A brief pause as a fresh thought occurred to him. 'She could have done it on the day she left – the Saturday.'

'How?'

'That Saturday there was an exhibition of books in the museum at Truro and I was on stewarding duty from one until six. I started out soon after twelve, leaving Morwenna to close the shop at half-past before she went off for her usual weekend.'

'I see. Did she know in advance that you would be away?'

'She could have done. It had been in the diary for weeks.' Simon hesitated before asking, 'What happens to me now?'

'Nothing at the moment, but you will probably be required to come to the station where you will be given an opportunity to make a fresh statement.'

Simon was shepherded back to the living room and a moment or two later DC Thorn joined them.

'This letter, sarge, tucked in amongst the books. It's signed "Tracey". Isn't that the name of the girl who spoke to the governor?'

They moved into the passage, out of earshot.

When Fox returned his manner was even more portentous. 'We shall take temporary charge of the books, the money and this letter. Of course I shall give you a receipt.'

'I don't know what to say.'

Although Meagor was a tall man, Fox could look down on him. 'As I said, we shall be in touch.'

It was almost dark when Simon, standing in his doorway, watched the police van manoeuvring out of the yard. He was about to go in when he saw his daughter coming towards him, caught in the path of light from the open door. 'Becky!'

She was carrying a hold-all. 'I heard it on the radio so I've come to keep you company for a day or two.' She reached for his hand and squeezed it. 'You're not safe on your own, Dad.'

His voice was unsteady. 'But what will your mother say?'

'To be honest I don't think she'll be sorry. I get on her nerves in the office.'

She glanced back at the alley which the police van had just left. 'What did they want?'

It was odd; the way in which her tone, her manner – her attitude – seemed to diminish both the intruders and their intrusion.

It was close to eight o'clock when Wycliffe arrived at the incident van. Kersey was there with Lucy Lane. Three weary people. The town was quiet but a few people loitered outside the tapes.

Kersey said, 'I had word from Fox earlier. He was on his way to the bookshop to go over the flat, "as instructed", he said.'

'He's a glutton for punishment, I'll say that for him.'

Wycliffe recounted his saga of the quarry edge, and Kersey was impressed. 'You think it could be murder?'

'We shall have to wait for the experts to tell us what to believe. Now, let's see where we stand.' Wycliffe made an effort to sound virile. 'Lucy! Presumably you arranged for the relatives to be notified and for the ID. What's the position?'

Unflappable Lucy took her time. 'I contacted the St Ives nick and Sergeant Hicks saw the aunt personally. Apparently she is disabled, but she has a companion who agreed to identify the body and Hicks was taking her to the mortuary. I've heard nothing since but there can hardly be a slip-up there.'

'And the cousin – Nicky?'

'I went to the squat in Carver's Ope where he's supposed to be hanging out. His mate, Pardon, was there with a girlfriend, but Barker had gone off somewhere. They claim not to know where, and they haven't seen him since Saturday. For what it's worth they say he's sure to be back.'

'If he doesn't turn up we'd better go after him but that's for tomorrow.'

Wycliffe yawned. 'We need to get back and organize a team. I want to be out of this tin box and into a pukka incident room. We also need accommodation for the team. But that means Shaw.'

Shaw was the squad's fixer.

Kersey seemed to wake up. 'Aren't you jumping the gun, sir? I mean, the chances are that it will still turn out to be suicide.'

Wycliffe was curt. 'You think so? Of course we don't know yet what Franks will say about the pathology but even if the girl killed herself we need to find out what happened to her during the time she was missing before she ended up in the quarry.'

Lucy Lane drove him home, and the ninety-minute journey was accomplished almost in silence. Lucy took the car on to her place and she would fetch him in the morning.

Helen and Ruth were playing Scrabble in the living room.

More than thirty years in the force had not taught him how to make a graceful transition from the sort of day he had just had to life at home.

He blurted out, 'The girl's been found dead in her car; in a flooded quarry.'

Helen said, 'It was on the news.' She knew that the less said, the better.

A shower, a drink, a prawn salad, and he felt almost human.

Tuesday 15 August

Wycliffe awoke but he did not immediately open his eyes; the sunlight was pink through his eyelids and he was still drowsy.

His first thought was, Morwenna is dead. And a moment later, Today is my birthday. In his half-awakened state he felt he ought to be able in some way to reconcile these two facts. Morwenna was twenty-three. I am fifty-four . . . He seemed on the point of reaching some profound conclusion but nothing came and he found himself thinking, Fifty-four years ago at six in the morning I was born in a farmhouse bedroom. Mother wouldn't go into a maternity ward . . .

Before that I didn't exist. There was a world without me . . . Now there is a world without Morwenna.

Where these thoughts might have led him he would never know for Helen spoke. 'Are you awake?' And

94

he opened his eyes. 'Happy birthday, darling!' was followed by a birthday kiss and the beginning of the day.

The birthday had already been celebrated but he was not allowed to forget it. Lucy came to fetch him as arranged. 'Happy birthday, sir.' And when he arrived at the office there was a vase of white and bronze chrysanthemums on his desk, with a card: 'Happy Birthday from the Team'.

Diane came in, looked at the flowers in simulated surprise and said, 'Well, well! I wonder who put those there?'

'Thank them for me; they're very nice.' He never felt adequate to these occasions.

Kersey was next. 'Like a greenhouse in here. Oh, I forgot, happy birthday, sir!'

Wycliffe was going through his mail and did not look up.

Kersey went on, 'I've had Fox on the phone. He's preparing his report after going over Meagor's place last evening.'

'Find anything?'

'The missing books and money stashed away in a cupboard behind Meagor's bed.'

Kersey had the satisfaction of seeing that he had Wycliffe's attention.

Wycliffe was recalling the little attic; the dormer window, the iron bedstead – and he thought he could remember a cupboard behind the bed, but wasn't sure. 'Did Meagor offer any explanation?'

'He said that the girl must have put them there.'

'Did he suggest why she would do such a thing?'

'Only that she could have done it on the assumption

that he would report his loss and be compromised when the stuff was found. Sounds weak to me.'

'Anything else?'

'The letter from the Tracey girl, which she told you about, advising Morwenna to get out while the going was good.'

Wycliffe sat back in his chair. 'Speaking honestly, Doug; doesn't all this strike you as a set-up? And a clumsy one, at that.'

They were interrupted by the Chief.

Oldroyd looked, as always, like a country gentleman who has dropped in for a chat before going on to something more interesting. A deceptive impression. 'So now you've got your redhead, Charles. What's the score? Suicide?'

'I'll know better when I've talked to Franks but I don't think the girl killed herself, and it certainly wasn't an accident.'

'Funny sort of murder.'

'But a reasonable way to dispose of a body.'

'I see. So it's a question of when, where and why? I don't know what it is about you, Charles, but you seem to attract the bizarre. Anyway, nice flowers! And a happy birthday if you can find the time.'

As the door closed Wycliffe and Kersey looked at each other. Kersey grinned. 'We shall miss him.'

Wycliffe could say amen to that. The next chief would be one of the still upwardly mobile. Oldroyd, through sound organization, a flair for personnel management and political nous, had been noticed in Olympus, making the job a possible springboard for the high-flier. Have-beens working out time till retirement need not apply.

＊　　　＊　　　＊

Wycliffe had a press call in the briefing room; the usual selection of bored professionals of both sexes, and a solitary TV cameraman. Wycliffe traced the story of the investigation so far, then took questions.

'Are you saying that the girl could have been murdered?'

'I am saying that we are waiting for reports from the experts. At the moment the evidence is inconclusive and we are keeping an open mind.'

'A suspicious death?'

'That sums it up. From what we know it is likely that the young woman met her death on the night of Sunday the thirteenth of August.'

'But she was missing for almost a fortnight. Is it likely that during that time she was being held against her will?'

'We have no evidence on that one way or the other.'

'Had she been raped or maltreated?'

'So far there is nothing to suggest anything of the sort but we are waiting for the pathologist's report.'

'Was the car's ignition switched on?'

'No, it was not.'

'The car was in gear?'

'No. It was in neutral and the handbrake was off.'

'So it's unlikely that she actually drove over the quarry edge.'

'It seems so.'

'Doesn't that contradict the possibility of suicide?'

'That is something for the experts to consider.'

'Was she dead at the time?'

'Again we have to wait for the pathologist to report.'

'Were there signs of a struggle?'

'No.'

The probing went on until they came to the inevitable question: 'Before her body was found there was a good deal of aggro directed against her employer. Is this likely to be relevant?'

'I've no idea at the moment of what may or may not be relevant.'

Then, winding down, 'Is there anything you would want us to do? Anything that might prove helpful?'

Beware of Greeks bringing gifts. Wycliffe was, but even the media has its uses.

'As always we shall be grateful for any help from the press. It is essential for us to establish this girl's movements during the fortnight she was missing as well as at weekends over the past six months. To that end I have arranged for copies of a fairly recent photograph to be handed around and we shall appreciate any publicity that is given to it.'

When the press had gone Wycliffe and Kersey were able to get down to planning, and an hour later Wycliffe, with Lucy Lane, was on his way. Kersey and the team to follow.

Another hot dry day. Wycliffe, Kersey and Lucy Lane were closeted in the larger of the two cubicles of the incident van, and though the windows were open to every stray movement of the air the van was like an oven.

Wycliffe, in shirt sleeves, felt sweaty and self-conscious. Lucy, in her discreet blue-grey frock, seemed cool and untroubled. Kersey oozed gently and didn't give a damn.

A team had been assembled: DS Fox, DCs Potter,

Dixon and Thorn, from headquarters, with variable assistance from the local force. DI Kersey in immediate charge.

Wycliffe steeled himself to breathe life into the inquiry.

'We still don't know what Franks will say about the pathology but I'm satisfied that the nature of the ground approaching the quarry edge and the fact that the engine was switched off makes suicide highly improbable. Of course the accident investigator will have his say, but in my opinion there's enough evidence to justify a suspicion of murder.'

Colours nailed to the mast.

The telephone rang. 'Dr Franks for you, sir.'

Wycliffe glanced at the others and muttered, 'Franks, on cue for once.'

'I heard that, Charles. I'm glad you appreciate how I look after you. This should have been my day off.

'About this redhead of yours. Of course she was dead when she entered the water.'

'And when was that?'

'I told you. Not more than twenty-four hours before they fished her out. The night of Sunday/Monday, the thirteenth and fourteenth of August. Will that do?'

'It fits,' Wycliffe grumbled. 'But it leaves a whole fortnight of the girl's life unaccounted for.'

'Your problem, Charles.'

'Next question: have you any idea of how she died?'

'Well, she had a more or less whole skin but, as you would expect, there was a good deal of bruising. Much of it probably came from being shaken about during the fall and from the shock of the impact. As I've told you often enough it's usually impossible to distinguish between ante- and post-mortem injuries.'

'But there are exceptions.'

'Don't prod me, Charles! Yes, and you may be in luck if that's what you want. There's an injury to the top of her head which caused cerebral damage without breaking the skin. It seems unlikely, strapped in as she was, that such injury was caused by the fall or the impact. Unlikely, but not wholly impossible.'

Franks paused to keep up the interest. 'However, it could have been caused by a blow from one of those blunt instruments we are all so fond of. I say *could*, no more than that.'

'A fatal blow?'

Franks havered. 'I don't think the injury, however it was caused, would have been fatal of itself. Sticking my neck out, if it was a blow, my guess is that she might have been knocked unconscious or into a dozy state amenable to handling.'

' "Amenable to handling." Charming way you have of expressing yourself, Franks. Delicate!'

It was an oddity in their relationship that while the pathologist always addressed Wycliffe as 'Charles', Wycliffe called him 'Franks'. There was an element of point-scoring; with Franks adopting the role of tutor, and Wycliffe refusing to play the dumb pupil.

'All right. Let me be clear. You are saying in effect that the girl could have been alive, though barely conscious, when she was put into the driving seat of her car, strapped in, and pushed over the edge. But that she was dead when she entered the water.'

'You're putting words into my mouth, Charles. All I've said is that your version is not impossible. But I'm not prepared to repeat that in court – not without a lot more to go on.'

'Simple question, then: what did she die of?'

'How about vagal inhibition? That was fashionable once. Now it's cardiac arrest. Everybody thinks they know what it means and they have it three times a week on the telly.'

'Any impression of her general health?'

A Franksian chuckle. 'Well, it wasn't very good when I saw her.'

Wycliffe was not amused.

'Anyway, no very obvious lesions. Incidentally, she wasn't a virgin, but how many girls of her age are? Think what it would mean for old rakes like me if they were.'

'Any evidence of maltreatment prior to the events leading to her death?'

'You're getting ponderous in your old age, Charles. The answer is, nothing obvious. But healthwise something did strike me, though I'm not going to talk about it until I've had a second opinion. Get hold of her GP and ask him if he knows anything.'

Wycliffe was piqued. 'Don't tell me anything you'd rather not.'

'I'll tell you whatever I can support with evidence, Charles.'

Wycliffe put down the phone and retailed the gist of this Franksian version. 'He's holding something back, but he suggests we should contact her GP. I suppose we can find out who that is through the Family Doctor Service. At least they'll tell us which bit of paper to ask for.

'One thing's sure; the evidence from pathology is at

least sympathetic to the notion that we are dealing with a case of unlawful killing and I propose to go ahead on that assumption.'

Kersey said, 'It's worth bearing in mind that the girl seems to have ended up in the quarry some time on Sunday night and that Meagor spends his Sundays with his sister at the farm, which can't be that far away.'

Wycliffe ignored him. 'Obviously we want to know everything there is to know about the girl and her background. We need to look into her life at St Ives where she went after her father's trial, and that's probably where we should start. Then there's the college at Camborne where she worked with her friend, Tracey.'

Lucy Lane had another approach. 'It seems to me that if she received a blow that rendered her virtually unconscious, it must have been before she was brought to the quarry. I mean, it's hardly likely that her killer enticed her there to look at the view.'

Wycliffe agreed. 'That quarry edge is conspicuous for miles around. The only possible privacy would be at night. In fact, it would make sense, as you say, if the girl was brought there, already in a semi-conscious condition, at some time during the night of Sunday/Monday.'

Kersey put in his bit. 'At which time her car must have been on the road, driven by the killer who, presumably, had to walk home.'

Wycliffe nodded. 'Forensic may be able to help when they examine her car, though I doubt it.' He summed up. 'For a start then, we lay on a house-to-house over the whole area. That is to say, within a two-mile radius of the village of Constantine. Let's start from the neighbourhood of the quarries and work south towards the river. We shall need help from Lister. See to that, Doug, and let's hope that for once somebody really has seen or heard something. A yellow Mini, and a man out walking in the middle of the night. We might get something. All reports to you.

'Then there are the dead girl's known routines. We're told that she regularly had her evening meal out. Obvious question: where and with whom? Scope for Potter, our resident foodie. Next, she was away every weekend. Where? Getting an answer there could be more difficult.' He patted his brow with a handkerchief that he hoped was clean.

Lucy Lane could not remember such a lengthy briefing from the governor. He was not given to such expositions. The case or the weather must have got to him.

But Wycliffe had not quite finished. 'Just one more thing – the good news, this time. Shaw thinks he can fix it for us to have a room in the former town hall – across the Moor from here.'

A package containing prints of photographs taken at the quarry ridge and of others taken of the body both at the scene and at the mortuary was delivered by a police motorcyclist.

The finding of Morwenna's body had featured in the previous night's radio news and now made the front page of the *Western News*:

'Dramatic Recovery. Missing Girl's Body in Submerged Car.'

This, of course, came before there had been any hint from the police of the possibility of murder. Now they had the morning's briefing to work on. The story was too good for them to pass up but he prayed that this was not going to be one of those cases that would inflame their imaginations.

He spread some of the newly arrived photographs on the table and looked them over. They were in three sets: the body, the vehicle and the terrain. He studied those of the ground near the cliff edge; the tyre marks had been cleverly enhanced, and two of the photographs gave a clear indication of the nature of the ground approaching the edge. Fox had done well.

Wycliffe got back to the programme: 'I'll take on the aunt at St Ives. Mr Kersey will allocate the rest.'

They had a pub lunch and when they returned to the van shortly after one-thirty there were preliminary reports from the vehicle examiner and from the accident investigator.

Three pages of technicalities were summed up in a statement from the vehicle examiner: 'I conclude that all significant defects in the vehicle, both structural and mechanical, may reasonably be attributed to the crash.'

Which surprised nobody.

The accident investigator was more interesting. With the support of his own photographs and diagrams the investigator gave his opinion:

'It is clear that the vehicle was stationary for some time at a distance of several metres from the edge. Bearing in mind that, on recovery, the ignition switch was off, and the gear lever was in neutral, it seems improbable that the vehicle was *driven* over the edge. The critical factor in determining whether or not the vehicle would, on release of the handbrake, have moved *of itself* towards the edge, must be the gradient and the nature of the surface. On-site observation shows that there is a slight upward slope towards the quarry edge so I have to conclude that the vehicle did not travel to the quarry edge on its own unaided momentum.'

Wycliffe took a deep breath. In other words, it must have been pushed. But never use one word where you can make do with six. Still, who's complaining?

'Phone for you, sir. A Dr Paul; says he was the girl's GP.'

The tentative voice and manner of a young man not yet totally dug in behind his professional defences. 'I've heard through the Family Doctor Service that you are making inquiries concerning the medical history of Morwenna Barker.'

'Yes. She's dead, perhaps murdered.'

'Exactly. Well, I am – was, her GP . . . My practice is in Camborne but I am free at the moment and it might be easier if I came to see you in Falmouth.'

'That would be helpful. We have an incident van on the Moor.'

'I could be with you in about half an hour.'

Service.

Dr Paul was tall, spare, athletic, and he wore a track suit to show that he was one of the boys. He had prepared himself and lost no time in getting to the point. 'Morwenna first came to me about eighteen months ago. She had left her aunt's place in St Ives and was living in Roskilly House, just outside Camborne; that's a small hostel which caters for students from Camborne College. You probably know that she was employed in the college library.'

The doctor did not fit into the constraints of the caravan; he wriggled uncomfortably on his bench seat as he tried to accommodate his legs under the table.

'She complained of a variety of symptoms which suggested a mild hypochondriasis. The poor girl had gone through a series of distressing experiences and a neurosis of some sort would hardly have been surprising. I did my best to reassure her and asked her to come and see me again. She did, in two or three weeks.

'By then certain of her symptoms had become more acute and there was an emerging pattern which suggested to me the possibility of multiple sclerosis. I referred her to a consultant neurologist and eventually that diagnosis was confirmed.'

Now and then the doctor glanced through the van window where cars were playing musical chairs in what the police had left of the Moor car-park. Was he experiencing that same sense of claustrophobia that usually afflicted Wycliffe in a doctor's surgery?

'What sort of a girl was she? How did she strike you?'

'I didn't know her well enough to make any sort of character assessment.' A prim disclaimer.

Wycliffe's response was brusque. 'You're not in the witness box, Dr Paul. You talked to the girl in circumstances which for her must have been exceedingly distressing. You're accustomed to dealing with people when their defences are down and all that puts you in a better position than most to say something intelligent about her. I only saw her once and then not to speak to.'

The young doctor flushed. 'If you put it like that, all

I can say is that she struck me as a very pleasant intelligent young woman who'd had the stuffing knocked out of her.'

Wycliffe grinned. 'That's better!'

'She blamed her disease on the traumatic experiences she had undergone, in particular, finding her father with his throat cut.' A brief pause to emphasize that he wasn't afraid of plain speaking. 'Then, by extrapolation, she blamed the man whose evidence had, in her view, set the whole train of events going by giving false evidence.'

'Is such an explanation feasible?'

'I haven't a clue.' The doctor was becoming increasingly human. 'I've no doubt specialists in the field would ridicule the notion, but specialists are like that. There are probably statistical data of some sort on which a judgement might be made if anybody ever got around to it.' Dr Paul sighed, no doubt reflecting on the labyrinthine complexities of medical science. 'Anyway, I gather that recent research suggests a genetic link.'

Wycliffe was beginning to like Doctor Paul. 'Anything else?'

'Another item that might be relevant. Shortly after hearing that she had contracted MS she came to me again saying that she was twelve weeks pregnant and asking for a termination. After discussing the case with my partner this was agreed and carried out.'

'Did she say who the father was?'

'No, she flatly refused to discuss that aspect.'

The young doctor and the ageing policeman had established a rapport and they parted on good terms.

'You've been a great help, doctor.'

'Anything I can do . . .'

With this behind him Wycliffe should have been in a better position to face the aunt. In fact, he was troubled by fresh doubts. All that he had heard made it easier to believe that the poor girl had killed herself. No-one who knew her history and understood the implications of the medical prognosis could doubt that she would have had motive enough.

So what was the hard evidence for murder? In the pathology, Franks had come up with the suggestion that a head injury *could* have been the result of a blow. The accident investigator had implied that the little car had probably been pushed over the edge.

The argument for murder rested on these two opinions plus a gut feeling. But Wycliffe had decided that, suicide or murder, his inquiry into the death of Morwenna Barker would, for the present, be treated as though it were a murder investigation.

Chapter Six

For Wycliffe, St Ives was a magical place and he thanked God that the cult of the theme park and amusement arcade had been out-manoeuvred by the arrival of the new Tate Gallery and what went with it. He prayed that the civic fathers and mothers of Penwith might in future begin to realize which side their bread is buttered.

There are two routes into the little town and Wycliffe chose the scenic, which culminates in a view of the bay through pine trees equal to anything the Med has to offer. A circuitous trip around the outskirts brought him back to the town centre and to the police station where there was an official car-park. 'Unauthorized vehicles will be clamped.'

In an elevated mood, Wycliffe muttered, 'Let 'em try it!'

Ardevera – House-by-the-Water – fronted directly on a narrow crooked street of undistinguished houses and small shops. Only initiates realize that the houses on the left side of the street back on to the sea.

The door was opened by a plump middle-aged woman who looked sadly in need of sleep.

'Miss Rowe?'

'Who wants to know?' She was agitated and there was an edge to her voice. Wycliffe showed his warrant card and introduced himself.

Her expression changed. 'Oh, you're police. I'm sorry. No, I'm not Miss Rowe, I'm Janie Mills; we live together. You'd better come in.'

He was shown into a room at the back of the house where only a walkway separated it from a tumble of black rocks and the open sea. In stormy weather the windows must have been drenched with spray.

The furnishings, including an impressive gilt-framed mirror over the fireplace, were survivals from an Edwardian middle-class home; comfortable to live with.

'I'm sorry that you had to be called upon to identify Morwenna.'

A brief nod. 'Yes, well, Molly couldn't do it, and Morwenna was more like a daughter to me. If you'll sit down, I'll fetch Miss Rowe.' She hesitated. 'She's very upset. I'm sure you'll be understanding.'

Piloted by Janie, Miss Rowe arrived in a wheelchair, a slim, slight woman with a surprisingly masculine voice. Her grey hair was streaked with remnants of the original red. A brown and white spaniel lolloped after her and spread itself at her feet like a miniature tiger rug.

'Molly Rowe. I'm Morwenna's aunt on her mother's side.' She held out a firm but arthritic hand. 'Yes, well, sit down. You can talk in front of Janie; she and I are like sisters and I've no secrets from her.'

Wycliffe apologized for disturbing them and offered sympathy.

'That *bookseller*!' Miss Rowe contrived to invest the

word with withering contempt. 'I can't think what made her work for him in the first place. After what he did to her father. And then to go and live with the man!'

Wycliffe had no brief to defend Meagor so he simply said, 'We want to find out more about Morwenna and her background and we need your help.'

'For heaven's sake, Janie, stop fussing with my cushion and sit down!' Miss Rowe was flustered but she made an effort to compose herself. 'All right, I'll try.' She adjusted her position in the wheelchair, grimaced with pain and went on, 'My sister, Bessie, was fifteen years younger than I.' A prim smile. 'I think my mother must have believed that she was past childbearing. At any rate, in due time Bessie grew up and married Barker, a fairly prosperous builder from around Mabe.'

Miss Rowe's lips expressed disapproval. 'They weren't really our sort of people. I mean, there was a nephew whom Barker more or less adopted when his parents died in a crash. The boy was in trouble before he left school and from what I hear he hasn't been out of it since.

'However, things seemed to go well enough with the marriage. Morwenna was born – a lovely child . . .' She smiled, and took ten years off her age. 'They let me choose her name and I called her Morwenna, which in Cornish means sea swallow. A charming name, don't you think?'

She pointed to a framed photograph of a teenaged Morwenna and a boy, perhaps a little older. 'There she is with Matthew.'

'Matthew?'

Janie explained. 'Matthew is my son. I'm a widow and we came here to live with Molly when my husband died. Matthew and Morwenna are the same age and they always got on well together.'

Miss Rowe resumed in her croaking voice, 'As I was saying, things seemed to go well enough with my sister's marriage until six years ago when Barker was arrested for manslaughter after a pub brawl. Then, largely on the evidence of that bookseller, he was convicted and sent to prison.'

Wycliffe sat in his black leather armchair and listened with flattering attention. The light flooding in from sea and sky made a great golden splash on the red Turkish carpet.

Miss Rowe continued, 'My sister with Morwenna, still a schoolgirl, came to live here with us. Barker served about half his sentence and was released on parole. He joined his family here.' She paused. 'No-one could say that I didn't do all I could for them.'

She looked from Wycliffe to Janie and back again as though challenging contradiction, then added, 'I have to admit I could find nothing whatever to complain of in the man's conduct. He had a reputation for a quick temper, but we saw no sign of it.'

She broke off to cough into a handkerchief. Janie, like a magician, produced an inhaler but was waved impatiently away. 'I think prison had broken him. He couldn't face the future and within a few weeks of coming here he killed himself.' Another pause while she again adjusted her position, her face distorted with pain. 'Actually he cut his throat in the upstairs bathroom. And, of course, it had to be Morwenna who found him.'

Janie said, 'Yes, it was a terrible thing to do in a house where he was a guest, and with his own daughter—'

Miss Rowe snapped, 'It's hardly likely that, having decided to cut his throat, the poor man was worrying about his manners.'

There was an appreciable interval while the only sound came from the snuffling of the sleeping dog, then Janie tried to fill the gap. 'Whichever way one looks at it, Morwenna was devastated. It was a ghastly experience. She was very fond of her father, in fact the three of them were close.'

Wycliffe made noises that were genuinely sympathetic.

Miss Rowe resumed. 'It's true that my sister never recovered. From then on she developed a heart condition which I am sure was brought on by the tragedy. There has never been heart trouble in our family – never! . . . However, Bessie died of a heart attack two years ago last June.'

Wycliffe allowed another sympathetic pause before asking, 'Was Morwenna employed while she was with you?'

'After leaving school she could have gone to university as Matthew did, but she chose to take a course at the college in Camborne and later she worked in their library. She was never the same after her father's death.'

'I suppose she had friends?'

'Until Matthew went to university they spent a lot of time together but there must have been others. She never brought them home but she had her little car and she was out most evenings and at weekends.'

'Was there a particular boyfriend?'

An arch little smile. 'Oh, I wouldn't know about that.' Miss Rowe said, 'She seemed such a sensible girl; she never gave a moment's worry while her mother was alive but after that she became terribly moody and unsettled . . .'

Janie Mills said, 'She left us not long after Bessie died and went to live in a sort of hostel with several other young people from the college. The poor girl needed fresh surroundings and company of her own age. I can understand how she felt.'

Miss Rowe nodded. 'I wouldn't argue with that. It was when she moved to Falmouth and went to work in that man's shop, the very man who . . . And then to move into his flat!' Miss Rowe was incapable of hiding her emotion.

'Did she keep in touch?'

Miss Rowe hesitated. 'While she was at the hostel, but I have to admit that after she went to work for that man I gave her to understand that she would not be welcome.'

A moment for reflection, then, 'That could have been very wrong of me.' She seemed to be confronted with a new and disturbing thought.

Wycliffe realized that the crunch had come. 'When she moved to the hostel, did you have any reason to think that Morwenna was unwell?'

'Unwell? There was nothing wrong with her to my knowledge.'

'I'm sorry to have to tell you that shortly after moving to the hostel she discovered that she was suffering from a serious illness.'

'What illness?' The words came in a demanding croak.

'I heard from her GP this morning that she was in the early stages of multiple sclerosis.'

'But—' Miss Rowe began to speak, and broke off. 'Oh, my God!'

'Poor child . . . Poor, dear child,' from Janie.

'Did she suffer?'

'I understand that the illness was in a very early stage but I will put you in touch with her doctor.'

'And she never told us!'

Wycliffe could not bring himself to mention the abortion. He said, 'Just one more question. I've heard that Morwenna had money and property. Is that correct?'

Miss Rowe was emphatic. 'Morwenna was a well-off young woman. She inherited property as well as money from her father; and her mother, who had money in her own right, left her a tidy sum.'

'I suppose you have no idea who handled her business affairs?'

Miss Rowe smiled. 'Bessie had a sort of accountant in Falmouth called Swaddling. She used to joke about him and his poky little office but she trusted him, and I doubt if Morwenna made any change. She didn't seem very interested.'

On the doorstep, as Janie was seeing him off, he said, 'Does your son live at home?'

'You could say that, I suppose.' A touch of bitterness. 'He got his degree but now, like so many others, he's looking for a job. We women aren't much company for him and he's off staying with friends mostly. He hasn't been the same since Morwenna went to work at the bookshop. They were very close in some ways.'

She added, after a pause, 'I don't know where he is at the moment but he does keep in touch – either he turns up or there's a phone call. He's got one of those caravan things, with a motor. It sleeps two. He bought it when he was a student and he and one of his pals went all over France in it.

'Of course he's more or less independent; his grandfather left him a tidy sum and he's not one to waste his money.'

'Good! Thank you for being so frank. When you hear from him will you ask him to get in touch with us? You've got the phone number and it's just routine.'

Outside in the crowded little street he found himself pondering on why it is that certain families seem to attract tragedy. Then he remembered a saying of his grandfather's, 'There but for the grace of God'. And he wondered why God was so discriminating with that commodity.

In the early afternoon Lucy Lane set out for Roskilly, the students hostel where Morwenna had lived, and she found it after a couple of misdirections. It was a large mid-Victorian house a mile or so out of Camborne towards North Cliffs. A short drive led to the front door, which stood open. Lucy recognized at once that bleak, rather scruffy anonymity which spells student lodgings.

A pretty dark girl was coming down the stairs. East Asian. 'You want somebody?' Her precise enunciation in English was so much more attractive than the slovenly garbled version now characteristic of the natives.

'I would like to speak to Mrs Lander.'

'She's in the kitchen. Debbie!' The girl raised her voice, and an answering call came from somewhere at the back.

'Somebody to see you.'

Deborah Lander, fortyish, a thin, fading, unfluffy blonde came down the passage, wiping her hands on a towel.

Lucy produced her warrant card. 'Detective Sergeant Lane.'

'Ah! I know who this is about. Let's go in here.'

Lucy followed her into a large room with a bay window. There were seven or eight battered armchairs and tables for pool and tennis.

'Find a seat. Of course it's the vac and I've only got two with me at the moment but there's twelve in term time.'

'About Morwenna Barker . . .'

Debbie swept back a straying wisp of hair. 'Yes. Poor Wenna! She left me nearly six months ago to go and work at that bookshop in Falmouth. Before that she worked in the college where my students come from. Of course she was older, and she didn't have much to do with them.'

'Can you tell me anything about her? How she spent her free time?'

'Well, mostly in her room, though towards the end she used to be away at weekends. Don't ask me where; she never gossiped like the younger ones. I mean, they tell Debbie everything.'

'Did she have visitors?'

'Only one – a chap about her own age. Quiet, wouldn't say boo to a goose. That's how he struck me anyway, but they used to spend a lot of time in her room and I don't suppose she was teaching him to knit.'

'Could you describe him?'

A sharp look. 'You don't think he had anything to do with what happened? Surely it was the man in the bookshop?'

'At the moment we've no idea who is or might be involved, but we do need to trace anyone who knew Morwenna at all well. A description would help.'

'Oh, yes, I see. You think he might be a witness or something. Well, I can try.'

Debbie composed herself to concentrate. 'He was on the tall side, but they all are these days. Five-ten or thereabouts. Thinnish, with brown hair . . . Don't they call it *en brosse*? And curly in front. I thought he looked pale – a bit peaky. No beard, moustache or sideburns – nothing like that.'

'That's a good description.'

Debbie looked pleased.

'Did she ever speak of this young man by name?'

'I don't think she spoke of him at all but I did hear her call him by name a couple of times – Matthew, it was. Yes, I'm sure it was Matthew.'

Matthew: Lucy experienced that lift which comes when two wires cross on a target.

'Can you remember, roughly, the last time he came?'

Debbie's brow wrinkled. 'It must have been some weeks before she left – long enough for me to think it was all over. Of course they had a row. I don't know what it was about but I heard Wenna shouting at the poor lad and when he came downstairs he was really upset. You could see from his eyes that he'd been crying.'

'Did she have her car here?'

'Oh, yes, a yellow Mini she used to call Buttercup. She used it every day to go to work.'

Lucy got up from her chair. 'I think you may have helped us. Could I see the room that was hers?'

'You can see it, but another girl took it over when she left. Not that it's changed much.'

The room was on the first floor and at the front of the house. A typical student's room though larger than most; functional, but spartan and shabby; now brightened by a couple of posters. An Oasis fan.

'Of course I could have made it a double, but Wenna paid a bit over the odds and the girl who's got it now isn't strapped for cash.'

Debbie went on as though it all came in a single breath. 'Nothing's changed except that Wenna had more books.'

Ten minutes later Lucy left. An above average morning, and she was mildly pleased with herself. Sometimes she wondered if in building her life around the job she was missing out on other things in a way that she would later regret: a proper home. A man, children . . . I live at second-hand. 'Dabbling my fingers censoriously in other people's lives.' Somebody said that – not about a policewoman, but as a job description it fitted well enough to pinch.

'But I'm not going to kid myself. Where would I be without it?'

Back at the incident van Lucy found Wycliffe muddling through a little heap of reports. It was rare for him to read anything consecutively, paragraph by paragraph, page by page and, in picking out a bit here and a bit there, he was a menace to any orderly arrangement of loose papers.

'Well, how did you get on?'

Lucy told him.

'So we have to get hold of the boy, Matthew. Apart from anything else he could well have been the father of the girl's aborted child. I was hoping not to add to his mother's troubles, but we may have no option.

'Anyway, it's less than twenty-four hours since the girl's death became public knowledge and he may not have heard it. Give him until the morning. If he hasn't put in an appearance by then, we'll go after him.'

Later that afternoon Nicky Barker arrived at the incident van and was interviewed by Kersey with DC Potter and PC Toms. Potter was a sound copper in situations not requiring even a ten-yard sprint, and Toms had been seconded from the local nick because he knew the town inside out and backwards. Kersey told them both to stay.

Barker's manner was aggressive rather than concerned. 'Your lot had good warning that the bookseller was up to something, and what did you do about it? Bugger all! I suppose you've got him banged up now it's too bloody late.'

It was hard to believe that Barker's genes had ever enjoyed even a nodding acquaintance with those of his cousin. His long white face, his small features, his black hair in a pony tail, were set off by the black shirt and jeans.

With a man like Kersey, Barker had misjudged his approach. Kersey studied him with exaggerated interest before speaking. Then, mildly, 'Of course we are very sorry about what has happened to Morwenna and you can be quite sure that we shall get to the bottom of it, but are you suggesting that Mr Meagor is responsible?'

'I'm not bloody well suggesting it, I'm saying that he killed her. He's a bloody pervert.'

'Presumably you can support your accusation with evidence?'

Barker made a vigorous movement expressive of disgust. 'What evidence do you want? It's obvious, it must be, even to your lot.'

Kersey had a way of dealing with suspects, aggressive witnesses and recalcitrants in general: a sustained expressionless stare. Lucy described it as ego shrinking and it had the advantage of being outside the scope of any practicable definition of intimidation.

When words followed the look they were usually mild, 'We can understand your concern, but accusations unsupported by evidence can land you in some difficult situations. We have started an intensive inquiry and you may be able to help us, but first, just for the record, tell us something about yourself. Where are you living, Mr Barker?'

'At the moment I'm sharing a place with a friend.'

PC Toms intervened. 'A squat in the Carver's Ope with Danny Pardon. He's a friend of ours too.'

Barker was about to protest but Kersey cut in, 'You were going to say, quite rightly, that your friends are no business of ours, so we'll let that pass. How long have you been in Falmouth? This time round, I mean.'

'Two or three months.'

'Working?'

'Not at the moment. But what's that got to do with anything?'

'When did you last see Morwenna?'

'A fortnight – nearer three weeks ago; I can't say exactly. We had a meal together.'

'And before that?'

'I think it was sometime in the previous week, but I'm asking for the second time, what's all this to do—'

'I'm sure you will understand that we need to know as much as possible about Morwenna's movements. When did you last see her before coming to Falmouth?'

'I can't say exactly but—'

DC Potter came in on cue. 'Did she ever visit you while you were inside?'

Barker looked from one to the other, hands clenched. 'So that's it! I'm being fitted up. My cousin has been murdered because of your bloody incompetence and you treat me like . . . like . . .'

'A toe-rag who knows the score?' Kersey looked up from a paper he seemed to be studying. 'We apologize, but you must admit it's a mistake easily made.' Kersey referred to his paper again, counting to himself, 'One, two, three . . .' He broke off, 'How old are you, Mr Barker?'

'Twenty-six.'

'And you've chalked up six convictions already, including two custodials.' Kersey ran down the list. 'Possession, possession with intent to supply, aggravated burglary, supplying Class C . . . Your stamping ground seems to have been Bristol; when did you leave home?'

'When my uncle got banged up. We never got on, but there was no room when he went.'

'Before you came back to Falmouth, how long was it since you'd had any contact with your cousin? Two years? Three? Five?'

'It was a long time.'

Kersey had given up any pretence of treating him as a bereaved relative. 'Was she the reason for this return to your roots? Perhaps you thought you might sponge on her.'

Barker was sullen. 'You can think what you like. I came because I stood a better chance of getting a job down here.'

'Did she give you money?'

Barker's little eyes were on Kersey, trying to decide how much of what he said could be checked. 'That's my business.'

'Roll up your sleeve.'

'Like hell I will! You've no right—'

'And you've no choice. Anyway it won't tell us anything we don't know. One look at you is enough. So get on with it.'

Kersey surveyed the scrawny arm. It was smooth. He tried to cover his blunder. 'Ah! Nil by needle, I see.'

'Very funny, Mr Kersey.'

Kersey snapped, 'What do you really know about what happened to Morwenna? Were you in on it? Is there something in it for you?'

It worked – more or less. 'God! I don't know anything! You can't say I had anything to do with it. I mean, she wanted me to help her and she paid me for it. That's all. It was a deal; I swear it! Hell! You can't say—'

Kersey cut in, 'Help her to do what?'

Barker collected his wits. 'She said that Meagor was a pervert, always pestering her.'

'Yet after working for him for two months she agreed to share his flat.'

'She said it didn't start until she was living there.'

'Did you really believe what she said about Meagor?'

A longish pause. 'He looks like a creep to me. I thought she might be trying to get something of her own back after what he did to Uncle. I hadn't much to thank her old man for but I would have been all for that.'

'What did she expect you to do?'

A slight shrug. 'Just to harass him a bit – put the story round, start the gossip, put through a phone call or two.'

'Smash his windows and daub his walls?'

'You can't prove I had anything to do with that.'

'And now Morwenna isn't here to tell us.'

Barker nodded. 'And I reckon Meagor must know something about that.'

Potter tried his hand. 'It seems that she spent very little of her free time in the flat. She must have had friends. For example she was away every weekend. Perhaps you can tell us where.'

'She told me nothing like that.'

'Talking about friends, yours in Carver's Ope say they haven't seen you since Saturday. Where've you been?'

Barker hesitated, 'That's my business.'

'Morwenna found her way into the quarry pool

some time on Sunday night. You don't happen to have been around then?'

Barker was shaken. 'My God! You really are trying to stitch me up. I was a fool to come here without a brief. Why should I want to hurt Wenna? She never did me any harm.'

'Perhaps you're in her will. Or if she never made one you could still be in for a share.'

Barker looked incredulous. 'You must be joking.'

'Think so?'

Kersey stood up. 'Anyway, we need a statement. DC Potter will take you to the nick where there are facilities.'

'Do I have a choice?'

'Yes. I expect Mr Meagor could be persuaded to make a complaint on which you could be charged with defamation and criminal damage, or we could decide to turn over your billet. Anyway, think seriously about where you've spent your weekends recently.'

That evening DC Potter made his tour of restaurants serving evening meals, looking for one that had been frequented by the dead girl.

After several blanks he struck lucky in a vegetarian place in Church Street, overlooking the harbour. Its clientele was an odd mix of the well-preserved elderly with a sprinkling of the young who still believed in tomorrow.

Potter watched them eating with the same mild surprise that he might have watched a Koala bear chewing away at his eucalyptus leaves.

He was immediately spotted as an intrusive carni-vore and pounced upon by the grey-haired headmistress-type who seemed to be in charge. 'Yes? Did you want something?'

Potter identified himself and produced his photograph of Morwenna surreptitiously as though it were a dirty postcard.

'Oh!' A quick look round to see that all was well, then, 'Come this way.' A little office about five feet square. 'Yes, I recognize the young woman.'

'She came here for her evening meal?'

'Most evenings – yes.'

'You didn't think to tell us?'

'Should I have done? I understood the police were looking for her, but as she wasn't here I felt I had nothing to contribute.'

'How often did she come?'

'Most weeknights – Monday to Friday.'

'Alone, or in company?'

The thin lips pouted. 'Well, she'd been coming here for several months; at first she was invariably alone, but after a while she was sometimes accompanied by a young man.' She added, with a thin smile, 'He seemed besotted.'

'You didn't recognize him?'

Hesitation. 'I did, as a matter of fact. It was Julia Meagor's son – Jonathan, I think he's called.'

'And you saw her with no-one else?'

'I don't keep a record of my customers' companions but I do remember that two or three weeks ago she came with a rather sinister-looking young man who seemed totally out of place here.'

Wycliffe's evening walks, whenever he was away from home, had become a tradition. None of his colleagues would have dreamt of offering to keep him company. He liked to prowl around the place where he happened to be with the notion (or excuse) that he might fit the people he had met and the things they had done into some sort of context. At a certain stage he would drop in at a restaurant or a pub for a meal or a snack as the mood took him. In fact, the whole exercise was a brooding session.

This evening, before setting out, he joined DS Shaw in the old town hall where the incident room was being laid out and equipped.

Behind the scenes of any major police investigation there has to be somebody responsible for logistics; in the army the job falls to the quartermaster; in Wycliffe's squad the quartermaster was DS Shaw.

The former town hall was a pleasant cream-painted building on the Moor, just around the corner from the bookshop. It dated from the time when local government meant a good deal more of what it said.

Shaw had acquired a large room (with the town arms still displayed high up on one wall) and a couple of small ones. Wycliffe discovered at once that it was easy to go in by the wrong door and end up in a café.

He brooded idly over equipment disgorged in chaos by Central Stores. There were trestle tables, VDUs with their keyboards, telephones, a terminal, a copier, a radio link – and paper; enough paper to lay the foundations for that edifice that might one day have to sustain the CPS and the courts. All this, and a coffee machine with plastic cups.

'Going well?'

'Ready by the morning, sir. By the way, the team is booked in at St Anthony's, a small hotel on Castle

Drive. Mr Kersey said you would want to be there too, so I've arranged that.'

Satisfied, Wycliffe left him to it. He had a fancy to explore the High Street area where something of the old town survived, remnant of the days when Falmouth was a packet station handling traffic with the major ports of the world. Halfway up the narrow high street, he came across a restaurant to his liking: 'Martha and Mary's: Good food, simply cooked'.

It was small, with nine or ten tables; and not flashy. The clientele seemed sober: couples having a quiet night out; even the birthday party, for whom two tables had been put together, celebrated discreetly. It was no more than two hundred yards from the bookshop.

A pleasant middle-aged woman with 'Martha' embroidered on her spotless white overall waited for his order and he could see Mary working in the kitchen.

'I'll have the beefsteak and kidney and a glass of chilled lager.'

When Martha brought his lager he asked, 'Does Mr Meagor from the bookshop ever eat here?'

The woman was not at all sure that she liked the question, but with a quick glance towards an empty table in an alcove she answered, 'Mr Meagor is one of our regulars, and a very nice gentleman he is, too.'

So there!

For Wycliffe the beefsteak and kidney was a treat denied him at home because Helen had her own ideas about healthy eating.

When he left the restaurant he set out on his walk; it took him up the rest of the hill and round the corner to Harbour Terrace. Wycliffe knew his Falmouth.

It was already dusk. Navigation lights dotted the harbour and, reflected in the sky beyond the docks, he could see the measured blinking of St Anthony's beam.

He came to a halt by a low wall convenient for the resting of arms. It was at such moments that he still regretted his pipe. Immediately below him were the roofs of Moor Street, to his left, the harbour, to his right, the Moor itself. A few yards from where he stood, a path broken by steps led down to the street and came out close to the bookshop.

Meagor's weekday world was laid out within this small compass. On Sundays he moved outside it to spend time with his sister and brother-in-law. Was that the whole scope of his present life?

Leaning on his wall Wycliffe juggled with names, phrases, visual snapshots and his own emotions, trying to discern the glimmerings of a unifying pattern. Was there one?

Meagor's part in Barker's trial, Barker's suicide. Morwenna seeking work at the bookshop and, after a time, moving into the flat. Morwenna's disappearance and the eventual discovery of her body. The cousin with a police record. The tricks played with the books and money . . .

Then the St Ives connection, Morwenna's health, her pregnancy. Matthew, the apparently wayward son of the self-sacrificing Janie. He and Morwenna had spent four of their formative years under the same roof and, according to Janie, they had got on well together. Morwenna had moved out and become pregnant or had become pregnant and moved out.

Money. Could money be involved? According to her

aunt, Morwenna was well off. Another job for Shaw; right up his street.

As he moved away from the wall to the steps he murmured to himself, 'It's complicated.' Wycliffe's conclusions after bouts of brooding rarely had the ring of profundity.

He looked at his watch. Shaw had booked him in at the hotel where the others were staying. Somebody would have seen to it that his meagre luggage was taken there, but he could not even remember what it was called.

The incident van had closed down for the night and he was on the point of telephoning the nick when he spotted a cruising patrol car and flagged it down. They would be strange coppers if they didn't know where the brass was spending the night.

'Yes, sir. St Anthony's on Castle Drive. Certainly, sir. A pleasure!'

Suitably embroidered it would make a good story for the canteen: 'We found him wandering in Moor Street – nearly brought him in. Hadn't a clue where he was. Didn't even know where he was booked. Is he going round the twist or has he always been like that?'

His reception at St Anthony's was cordial. Dinner was over, 'But we can put on a tasty cold meal.'

'Thank you, but I've already eaten.'

Kersey, Lanyon and Potter were in the bar. Wycliffe said, 'My round. Where's Lucy?'

'Catching up on her beauty sleep.'

'It seems to work for her; perhaps we should try it some time.'

Kersey said, 'Potter's gone all vegetarian. He's

found the place where the girl went for her evening meal. Tell the Super, Potter.'

Potter told his story. 'It looks as though she was seeing the Meagor boy on a more or less regular basis, sir.'

Wycliffe awarded the official pat on the back. 'We'll follow that up in the morning. Anything else?'

'Yes, sir. One evening, not long ago, the girl had a different companion, another young man: "Sinister and quite out of place", according to the lady in charge. Sounded to me, sir, like a fair description of our Nicky. He'd be out of place anywhere except inside.'

Wycliffe said, 'I haven't met him, but you've had a good evening. Pity you're not a vegetarian, Potter.'

A phone call to say goodnight to Helen.

'You're not using that mobile thing of yours?' Helen took health scares seriously.

'No, I'm on the house phone.'

Wycliffe was intrigued by the facility with which modern man (and woman) can contract diseases from unlikely sources. It was not so long since he had come to terms with the notion that he might not be entirely safe from his cat, now he wondered how long it would be before somebody picked up a computer virus, and what the symptoms might be.

'What's the hotel like?'

'It seems very comfortable and they tell me there's a sea view, but I haven't looked yet.'

Chapter Seven

Wednesday 16 August

Wycliffe had not drawn his curtains and he had only to raise his head to see out of the window. To his left and quite close, Castle Point and the coastguard station. Then nothing but the level plain of the sea, glittering; dazzling in the morning sun.

Seven o'clock, Wednesday. Forty-eight hours ago Morwenna Barker's body was still in her little car at the bottom of the quarry pool.

A troubled night. A good bed had been unequal to the events of those forty-eight hours. Bad dreams had dredged up distorted images from the labyrinth and now, tired and moody, he faced a new day.

Kersey and Lucy Lane were already down. Lucy was having her usual fruit juice and toast, while Kersey was halfway through his bacon, egg and sausage.

Wycliffe ordered cornflakes, toast and coffee.

Kersey said, 'You'll probably live to be a hundred and two, sir. At least it will seem like it.'

Half an hour later they were gathered in their new quarters, in the box-like room which would be Wycliffe's office for the duration. There was a newspaper on his table with a front-page photograph of the dead girl under a heading:

'WAS MORWENNA MURDERED?'

Morwenna, the redhead, had become a household name.

Already it was hot in the little room and Kersey grumbled.

Lucy said, 'According to the forecast the weather is breaking up. Rain this afternoon.'

Wycliffe ran a finger around the inside of his collar. 'It can't be too soon for me.

'Anyway, let's get started. I want to know more about Morwenna's affairs – sexual and financial. According to her aunt, she was well off. Shaw looks and thinks more like an accountant than a policeman, so put him on it. Then there's young Meagor who, it seems, joined her most evenings for her meal. We need to talk to him. And we have another young man, the ubiquitous Matthew. It's time we got after him.'

Kersey and Lucy Lane left and Wycliffe was settling down to the reports when he was interrupted. 'A Mrs Julia Meagor to see you, sir.'

Wycliffe did a mental double-take and came up with Simon Meagor's wife.

He wondered what to expect and went to meet her. 'Superintendent Wycliffe.'

'I'm Julia Meagor, Simon's separated wife.'

No trimmings. She was lean, angular and blonde-turning-grey; aged late forties to fifty; voice and manner, crisp and businesslike.

Wycliffe resisted any tendency to become mildly flustered. This woman could have that effect.

He escorted her to his over-sized cupboard and as soon as she was seated she began: 'Let me make my position clear. I'm here as Jonathan Meagor's mother. Jonathan is nineteen and he remained with me when I separated from my husband ten years ago.'

'I see.' At least one could be non-committal.

'This morning I had a telephone call from an acquaintance who runs a vegetarian restaurant in Church Street. She told me that the police had been making inquiries there concerning the girl whose body was found in the quarry. It seems that she had her meal there most evenings, and that my son was often in her company.'

Having established the parameters she sat back in her chair. 'I am here to get this sorted out.'

Wycliffe roused himself from an unproductive attempt to imagine this woman sharing a bed with Simon.

'We do need to talk to your son, Mrs Meagor. Anyone who had contact with the dead girl shortly before her disappearance could be an important witness.'

A quick nod. 'Or even a suspect. You've no need to try to disguise the situation from me, superintendent.'

'But your son is of age and it is his obvious responsibility to come here himself, not to allow you to do it for him. Have you spoken to him?'

'No, I have not, but I fully understand the position. His association with the girl only came to my knowledge this morning. Jonathan is a student at the local art college and he is on vacation at the moment. He has been depressed recently and yesterday I persuaded him to accept an invitation from a friend in Plymouth to stay for a couple of nights. I will see that he's back in the morning and you can depend upon it that he will report to you here.'

Wycliffe thought, In chains if need be. But at least she was being co-operative.

She got up from her chair, terminating the interview, then had second thoughts. 'Perhaps I am allowed to add that neither my husband nor my son would be capable of violence of any sort against anybody. I have lived with both long enough to be quite certain on that score.' She sounded vaguely regretful.

A pause, then a further addendum: 'And as to my husband enticing or forcing this girl into bed with him – the very idea is ludicrous! You can take it from me, Simon is a victim of malicious gossip, superintendent.'

Wycliffe saw her off the premises and came back wondering what sorting demon had been responsible for that particular pairing off of the sexes.

The first reports from the house-to-house were coming in. The team had concentrated on the countryside around the quarries north of the village, and Lucy was leafing through them.

Wycliffe turned up to peer over her shoulder. 'Anything?'

'Only this, so far. It comes from a woman living between the village and the quarries.'

Lucy read the verbatim report aloud. ' "Looking out of my bedroom window at some time during the night of Sunday/Monday I saw a small light-coloured car, probably a Mini, coming from the direction of the village. I think it must have been between one and two in the morning. The car was being driven fairly fast and it had only its sidelights on. I couldn't see who was in it." '

Lucy, pencil poised, referred to a map spread on the table. 'The map reference puts the woman's house on the B 32912, about a mile to the north of the village, and within a half-mile of the quarry.'

Lucy's pencil followed the road westward. 'And there's *Trevathick*. Isn't that the Bunts' farm – where Meagor goes on Sundays?' She shifted the map so that Wycliffe could see. 'That car must have passed the farm only a few hundred yards before the woman saw it.'

Wycliffe was interested. 'We may have something there. If it was our Mini . . . As to the Bunts, we could do with knowing a bit more about them anyway. But first I want a word with Meagor and I think it's time he made Mr Kersey's acquaintance.' He added, with a grin, 'Don't you?'

Lucy said, 'I don't even speculate on such matters of high policy, sir.'

The bookshop displayed the 'Closed' notice but the china shop was in business. Through the window Wycliffe could see a customer being attended to by a young woman.

Wycliffe said, 'Ten-fifteen, coffee time; we may find Meagor in the market. Let's see.'

Kersey was intrigued. Because of his rank it was some time since he had accompanied Wycliffe on one of these fishing expeditions, and this brought back memories. 'You haven't changed, sir.'

'You mean that I'm still poking about like a DC, and you're right. A DC works hands-on and that suits me. There are only two snags: one is that you have to take orders from everybody else; the other is the pay.'

Wycliffe liked markets and this one, with its glass roof, was bright and cheerful, filled with a potpourri of smells. A café with a circular counter surrounded by tables occupied a central position. Mid-morning; the market was busy. Housewives battled through the aisles with their bags, buggies and children, plus the occasional husband trailing behind. A few took the weight off their feet at the café tables.

At one of the tables Wycliffe spotted Jeremy Scott with two companions.

Wycliffe said, 'Meagor isn't here.'

Kersey turned to leave but Wycliffe went to the table and pulled out a chair. 'All right if we join you?'

A nasty look from Burrows as he turned to indicate an empty table close by, but Scott cut in, 'This is Superintendent Wycliffe, Eddie.' And for Wycliffe's benefit, 'Simon isn't with us this morning, Mr Wycliffe.' He held out his hand. 'Jeremy Scott – china.' The fat man had an air: the industrial magnate from the Potteries.

Introductions were brief. Simms, the wizened little jeweller, said, 'Pleased to meet you both.' Burrows said nothing.

They were interrupted by a bare-armed Amazon who pitched on Wycliffe, 'You're in his place. Do you want his coffee and chocolate biscuit?'

'I'll have a coffee, and one for my colleague.'

It was an experience to Wycliffe's taste. To appreciate

its full flavour he would have preferred it without Kersey but one can't have everything.

He could read Kersey's thoughts. Where does he think this is getting him? The answer was probably nowhere, but just as when he read somebody's diary or journal, he was living a bit of another man's life, getting under his skin. If, as he sometimes imagined, he had been in Meagor's shoes, would he have been a regular with this little group, drinking his coffee, eating his chocolate biscuit and taking stock of the world?

Why not? It was a life.

Scott said, 'We've been talking about Simon; he didn't open up this morning and I phoned him. He said he didn't open because he had so much work to catch up.'

Simms said, 'He's depressed.' A deep sigh. 'Now he knows that the girl is dead – well, I wouldn't be surprised if he did something drastic. The whole business has been getting him down.'

Burrows placed his coffee cup in the saucer and became judicial. 'He spends too much time brooding. Always been the same. His daughter was with him yesterday, but I doubt if she'll stay on. Women can plague a man but when the crunch comes you need somebody.'

Wycliffe said, 'I suppose it makes a change for him at the weekends when he goes to his sister at the farm.'

Jeremy Scott nodded. 'You could say that but neither of the Bunts would be my choice to spend much time with.'

Burrows said, 'Mine neither. Bunt is a queer one, a

dark horse and tight-fisted. What's more, he didn't do his mate any favours when it came to the trial.'

'His mate?'

'Barker. They was in it together.'

Little Simms chuckled. 'You got to admit that Timmy Roach took 'em both for a ride, though he didn't live to enjoy it.'

Burrows said, 'I don't hold no brief for what happened to Roach, but he was a scumbag in any language.'

Wycliffe stirred the mix: 'The Barkers lived near the Bunts at one time, didn't they?'

Burrows said, 'Near enough. Just across the road.'

'Didn't this man Roach get killed in a scuffle with Barker?'

'That's what the jury said.'

Scott chipped in. 'On evidence from Simon, backed up by Bunt – his brother-in-law.'

Simms looked worried. 'We mustn't give the Super a wrong impression. The fact that we don't have much liking for Bunt, is not to say we think the jury got it wrong.'

Wycliffe was becoming increasingly convinced that the Barker trial and what led to it could be crucial to an understanding of much of what had happened since.

He drank his coffee. It was soon over; too soon for his liking. As they were leaving he said to Kersey, 'Interesting, don't you think?'

But Kersey held his peace.

Just beyond the iron grille which was closed at night there was a gap in the wall giving access to the yard where Meagor parked his van. They could see the bookseller through the office window, sitting at his desk, quite still.

As they approached, Meagor saw them, left his desk and came to open the door.

He was nervously apologetic. 'I'm catching up on things. I thought I would close the shop for the morning and see what I could do about it.' He looked from one to the other then added, almost as though challenging them, 'My daughter Becky has been with me since Monday night and she's going to stay for a while. She's just gone out to buy a few things.'

Wycliffe introduced Kersey who received a nervous scrutiny. 'You should know that we are treating Morwenna's death as possible murder.'

They sat around the desk where Wycliffe had seen Morwenna working at her ledger, enveloped by her red hair. He produced one of the prints he had brought with him and passed it across to Meagor. In the photograph Morwenna's body was still in the driving seat of her little car, her head resting on the steering wheel which was draped by her hair, hair that was now lank and dripping.

'That's how we found her. It seems likely that she was bundled into the car after being stunned by a blow to her head. Then, whoever was responsible could have pushed her car over the quarry edge.'

For reasons that were not altogether clear to himself Wycliffe was treating the bookseller to a dose of reality.

Meagor said, 'It's terrible, but there's nothing I can say. I don't know where Morwenna spent her weekends, and I know of no-one who could possibly have wanted to harm her. I can only say again that I think she must have come here to stir up trouble for me because she believed that I gave false evidence against her father. And she went off without a word to embarrass me further.'

Meagor made this statement as though it had been prepared in advance. His hands were trembling as he fiddled with the papers on his desk and his manner was sullen. 'I've told you all I know.'

Kersey cut in, 'What about the books and the money which, it seems, never left the premises?'

Meagor sat back in his chair with a deep sigh. 'How can I explain something which I don't understand myself?' For the first time Meagor was showing fight. 'Morwenna *must* have hidden them there.'

Wycliffe was soothing. 'Very well, Mr Meagor, let's get back to your evidence in that trial. When we last talked I asked you whether at the time of the Barker trial, or since, you've had any doubt that Morwenna's father was justly convicted. Your answer was evasive.

'Now you say that Morwenna's purpose in coming here was to humiliate you in revenge for your part in her father's conviction. Now Morwenna is dead, perhaps murdered, and I have to know more of the circumstances surrounding that trial. Do you maintain that the evidence you gave was wholly true?'

Meagor seemed incapable of sitting still and his features were contorted as though he suffered physical pain.

Wycliffe said, in a voice that was almost gentle, 'You'll have to face this sooner or later.'

At last it came. Meagor spoke in a low voice with long and frequent pauses as though he were reliving the events he described. 'It was after the Traders dinner . . . I was ill . . . Ever since I can remember I've suffered violent digestive attacks if I eat certain foods and take alcohol at the same time . . . As I went through the Gents to the cubicles there were two men with their backs to me in the stalls.'

'Did you recognize these men?'

A long pause. 'The light was poor, but one of them was Timmy Roach. You couldn't mistake Timmy; he was small and he was gabbling away as usual in his high-pitched voice.'

'And the other?'

'I thought the other was George Barker.'

'You thought that *at the time*?'

Meagor shook his head. 'I can't be absolutely certain, but I must have . . . I was violently sick in the cubicle and I remember hearing Timmy's voice raised as though there was a quarrel. The other man was speaking, but quietly, so that I couldn't hear what he said.'

'Go on.'

'Suddenly there was a noise like a loud smack; somebody cried out, and there was a sort of thud. I opened the door as soon as I could and there was Roach, his head in a pool of blood, on the tiled floor.'

Meagor stopped speaking and began to fiddle with the papers on his desk.

'Did you see a man leaving?'

'Yes, I did, but only his shoulder and arm as the door closed. I thought it was George Barker.'

'You thought that *at the time*?'

Another shake of the head. 'Yes, because I had taken it to be him with Roach when I came in.'

'What did you do?'

'I stooped over Roach but there was nothing I could do. I think I shouted and Arthur Bunt, my brother-in-law, came in.'

'Could it have been someone else with Roach in the first place?'

Meagor hesitated. 'I suppose it could have been.'

'All right, carry on.'

'Afterwards Arthur told me that just before I raised the alarm George Barker had rushed out of the Gents, pushed past him and out into the street like a mad man.'

Meagor's voice had dropped so low that he was scarcely audible. He added after a pause, 'I thought I did right at the time.'

Wycliffe said, 'I am not saying that you deliberately misled the court but is it possible – *possible*, that your evidence was mistaken?'

Meagor hesitated, then, 'I have to say yes, to that.'

On their way back to the incident room Kersey said, 'You can't help feeling sorry for the poor bastard. I think he could be talked into almost anything. But if the jury did get it wrong, and it wasn't Barker who killed the little fellow, then it must have been this chap Bunt. After all, he said he saw Barker come rushing out of the Gents just before—'

Wycliffe cut him short. 'Exactly. We must hear the Bunt version.'

But Kersey was not easily silenced. 'On the other hand our business is with a dead girl, not with a manslaughter trial that might have taken a wrong turning six years ago.'

Wycliffe was irritated. 'It seems to me that we might find difficulty in separating the two.'

Back in the incident room he brooded over the map: the quarry, Bunt's farm, the house of the nightwatcher who had spotted a little car, and now the house where Morwenna was born. All of these could be enclosed within a circle whose radius was little more than a half-mile. It was suggestive, but of what?

And another question: during the fortnight that Morwenna was missing, had she been constrained? Or was she, as Meagor believed, deliberately absenting herself to cause him further embarrassment?

Wycliffe was acutely aware that he had put himself out on a limb. By his use of manpower as well as by the nature of his inquiries he had committed himself to a murder investigation. Oldroyd was indulgent but he too had to account for the deployment of his resources.

The finding of a chronically sick girl in her little car, in a quarry pool – haunt of her childhood – hardly needs to be dressed up as murder on the strength of a single cranial injury of dubious provenance. Old-timers like Wycliffe had to learn that police work must be cost effective, which, being interpreted, means that any investigation with the whiff of a possible blind alley about it must be avoided.

But how many killers are never even questioned?

Chapter Eight

Shortly after twelve, with Lucy Lane driving, Wycliffe was back in granite country. For centuries Cornwall has had its entrails ripped out for tin, copper, granite and china clay. Three of these have fallen upon hard times but the spoil heaps of all four litter the countryside.

Higher Argal, Lamanva, Treverva – two days earlier they had followed the same route to witness the recovery of Morwenna's car and body from the quarry pool. They passed the track that led off in the direction of Job's Pit and a little later, at the very top of a steep rise, they came to Trevathick Farm, home of the Bunts.

Lucy pulled in by a freshly painted white gate from which a short gravelled drive led up to a trim farmhouse. They left the car and walked up the drive. House and garden had been kept strictly separate from the farm. In front of the house a large shaggy Alsatian held an heraldic pose in readiness for some invisible camera; it had no time for them.

A woman answered their knock.

'Mrs Bunt?' Wycliffe introduced himself and Lucy.

Mrs Bunt was lean, inclined to be waspish; not

much to suggest a parentage in common with Simon. 'We were just about to sit down to our meal but, I suppose, if it's about the girl . . .'

'I would like to speak to you and your husband.'

In an old-fashioned sitting room, overstocked with furniture and ornaments, they waited, and were eventually joined by the man himself.

Bunt was not big, but brawny, a hands-on farmer moulded by hard work; dirt under his fingernails. A type of Cornishman, not conspicuously bright, but as artful in working the EC handouts as any of his Euro counterparts. His manner was terse.

'Has something happened to Simon?'

'No. I've come here because it could be easier to talk to you about certain things than to him.'

'Such as?'

'We shall come to that.'

Wycliffe was looking out of the window. The scene was apocalyptic. Towering masses of blue-black cloud were creeping up the sky from the south-east, while at one point a shaft of sunlight directed a theatrical spotlight on to a grey-green mound of discarded granite blocks.

Bunt came to stand beside him. Wycliffe said, 'That ridge, surely that must be the one above Job's Pit?'

'That's it; that's the quarry where your people found her.' He spoke in a low guttural voice like an articulated growl.

'You must have had a grandstand view.'

'We knew something was going on but we had no idea what.'

Mrs Bunt said, 'Can't we sit down?'

Lucy and Wycliffe were given chairs on either side

of the empty grate while Mrs Bunt sat on an upright chair near the door. Her husband remained on his feet.

Wycliffe said, 'You may have heard already that there is a strong possibility that Morwenna was murdered. In my opinion there are grounds for thinking that her conduct, and what happened to her may have had something to do with her father's trial for manslaughter, his conviction, imprisonment, and subsequent suicide. I understand, Mr Bunt, that you were at that Traders dinner on the night of the incident and that you testified at his trial.'

'Just to what I saw.'

'And that was?'

Bunt, a man never likely to be caught offguard, took his time. 'The dinner was over, most people had gone home. It was raining and I was waiting in the vestibule for a taxi. Barker came out of the Gents like a wild man. He rushed past me without a word and out of the door into the rain.'

Bunt spoke in staccato phrases with pauses between. 'I was on the point of calling after him when Simon came out, looking like death. He said, "Come quick! Roach is dead!" I went into the Gents and saw Roach lying on the floor in a pool of blood. I shouted to Simon, and a couple of others who had turned up, to call an ambulance but I knew it was too late. Roach was dead right enough.'

Bunt paused before adding, 'That's what I saw and heard and that's what I told the court.'

Wycliffe said, 'I've talked to your brother-in-law and he is not absolutely certain that it was Barker he saw leaving the scene that night, so the positive identification rests on your evidence.'

Bunt looked at Wycliffe with suspicion. 'I don't know what you're after, mister, but I do know what I saw. As far as Simon's concerned, he seemed sure enough then. What he says now is up to him.'

Mrs Bunt intervened. 'Simon's my brother and I've never known him tell a deliberate lie, but he can be talked out of anything. I dare say you've been putting pressure on him; you and that girl. It's not right! She came here . . .'

A black look from her husband and Mrs Bunt broke off but it was too late.

'Morwenna Barker came here? When?'

Bunt was sullen. 'A week or so before she went missing. She said she wanted to clear her father's name, but it looked to me as though she was trying to blacken mine.'

As they talked the room had darkened and now the sun was blotted out. Faces looked pale in the grey light; colour was bleached from the landscape.

Wycliffe decided on a different approach. 'I understand, Mr Bunt, that you and Barker were involved in a housing project that was frustrated by Roach.'

Bunt was preparing his answer when his wife intervened. 'Arthur was a fool to get mixed up with the Barkers. I knew no good would come of it.'

Her husband started to protest but she cut him short. 'You've had your say for long enough, Arthur, now it's my turn. George Barker was drunk, and in one of his tantrums he killed Roach. Of course that put paid to any chance there might have been of doing a deal over access, and I can't say I was sorry, though it cost us.'

'And as it happened, your brother, Simon, was a key witness for the prosecution,' Wycliffe intervened.

'Yes, but whatever you've persuaded him to believe, all Simon did was to help put George Barker where he belonged. And that girl, Barker's daughter, was set on making him suffer for it. Simon is soft; he shouldn't have let her inside his shop door.'

'And now she's dead – probably murdered.'

'Maybe, but I'm quite sure it was none of Simon's doing.'

Lucy Lane, who had not spoken before, said, 'You see your brother as a victim?'

The woman gave Lucy a look of critical appraisal before deciding that she might be worth talking to. 'Of course I do! From the beginning that girl has played with Simon like a cat with a mouse. And your lot have been ready enough to dance to her tune.'

Bunt looked troubled, but his wife went on, 'You're strangers to these parts; you don't know us Cornish, any of us. The Barkers have never been up to much. Look at that Nicky, the girl's cousin – in and out of prison. His grandfather was the same—'

Bunt intervened. 'There was never anything against George.'

Mrs Bunt made a disparaging gesture. 'He was never in gaol, I'll give you that. Maybe he was too smart; but there were other things.' She hesitated, then seemed to make up her mind. 'When George Barker was in his twenties and without a penny to his name he seduced Bessie Rowe, a girl of sixteen from a good family in St Ives. The Rowes weren't having any; they hushed the whole thing up as far as they could; a private nursing home, and the poor kid was adopted almost before it opened its eyes.'

Wycliffe said, 'But surely George Barker married a Bessie Rowe.'

He received a knowing look. 'Ah, so you do know that much. The silly girl was besotted, and when she was twenty-one and got control of her money she married Barker.'

Bunt was uncomfortable. 'But you got to admit that by then George had his business and was making a go of things. Even the Rowes accepted him in the end.'

His wife snapped, 'They didn't have much choice, did they?'

Wycliffe, diplomatically, changed the subject. 'I gather that Simon spends Sundays here.'

'Every Sunday. I make sure the poor man gets one good meal a week.'

Wycliffe tried another tack. 'It seems that Morwenna was away for the whole of each weekend; you've no idea where she went?'

'No, but when you find that out you'll find there's a man behind it.'

'If you will think back to last Sunday fortnight, the weekend that Morwenna disappeared, did your brother come as usual?'

'Of course! He never missed.'

'And last Sunday?'

'As usual.'

'Can you tell me at what time he left?'

'He always leaves at about the same time, eight or just after.'

Wycliffe was fishing with no real object in mind and he was getting near the knuckle. He changed his tactics. 'The fact that Morwenna's car, with her in it, went over the edge into Job's Pit suggests that she spent her weekends and probably the fortnight she was missing somewhere near here.'

Mrs Bunt was quick to see a possible implication. 'I don't know about that. All I can say is that Morwenna knew the place well. When they married, George Barker and his new wife bought Chygwyn, along the road a bit from here. You can guess who put up the money for that. Anyway, even when Barker decided that his business would do better in Falmouth, they didn't move house. They only left after he was sent to prison, and Morwenna must've been sixteen or seventeen then. That's when Bessie decided to go back to St Ives and live with her sister.'

Enough to be going on with. To the obvious relief of the Bunts, Wycliffe got up to leave.

On their way out Wycliffe asked Bunt about the Barkers' former house.

'A couple of hundred yards down the hill, back the way you've come, on the other side of the road. You can't miss it.'

Just off the brow of the hill, Lucy said, 'This must be it, the Barker house on one side, and a couple of cottages on the other.' They parked by the cottages and almost opposite a house, standing alone, overlooking the valley.

Lucy looked at the map, 'Unless I'm mistaken, one of those cottages must be the home of Mrs Pearce, the lady who keeps obo at two in the morning. Shall we have a word with her?'

'After we've had a look at the house.'

They got out of the car and walked across. A 'For

Sale' notice secured to a pole was propped against one of the gate posts.

It was a strange countryside; a barren moorland cut into by fertile valleys. The sky was blue-black and louring and by contrast the green of the valley seemed strangely bright.

Chygwyn was well built and agreeably sited but in no way special.

Lucy said, 'Is this what we came out in the wilderness to see?'

Wycliffe said, 'When Barker arrived here with his new wife he must have felt that he really had his feet firmly on the ladder.'

And a moment or two later he murmured, 'So this is where Morwenna was born.'

Lucy looked at him with affection. 'You're a strange man. Sometimes it seems to me that you've taken these people into your life.'

It was starting to rain in earnest; lightning flickered across the valley and thunder grumbled away threatening worse to come.

Wycliffe said, 'Let's pay a visit to your night-watcher.'

They picked the right one out of two. 'Mrs Pearce?'

A slim dignified lady with silvery grey hair cut in a short bob, deep brown eyes and a smooth, tanned complexion.

Wycliffe introduced himself and Lucy.

'Ah, the police. Would you like to come in?'

A small sitting room with good, plain, serviceable furniture, and three or four framed watercolours on the walls.

'Do sit down. I imagine you've come about what I

told your policeman, but I'm afraid I can't add anything to what I said.'

'You've lived here for some time?'

'For almost ten years. I came here when my husband died because it was cheap.' A thin smile. 'And I got to like it.'

'So you would have known the Barkers when they lived opposite?'

'Of course. We were neighbours. Theirs is a sad story. That poor girl on top of the rest.'

'You must have known her as a schoolgirl.'

'Indeed. A very pleasant one; always a smile. And she grew into a beautiful young woman, only to come to this.'

'You've seen her sometimes – since the Barkers left?'

'Very rarely. On two or three occasions I've spotted her across the road there, presumably on nostalgic visits. Not that we've spoken. I don't expect that she wanted to renew an old anquaintance and I can understand that.'

Lucy asked, 'Can you remember when you last saw her?'

A frown. 'Several months ago. It was winter, though as I remember quite a nice day. The house was for sale then, as it is now, and it happened that her visit coincided with someone else's, a young man who seemed to have an interest in the property. I thought it was a chance encounter but after a while they went off together – walking. I was surprised. They must have returned later to their cars which were parked on the hill.'

Mrs Pearce looked down at her long bony hands.

'You will think that I do nothing but gaze out of my windows.' A quick smile. 'I shall, of course, deny that, but living alone as I do, the smallest incidents can become memorable.'

Wycliffe said, 'You were surprised that these two young people seemed to be on such friendly terms. Do you mind telling me why?'

Mrs Pearce seemed mildly embarrassed. 'I suppose I'm not a very politically correct person, but Morwenna looked so lovely with her mass of red hair catching the sunlight; while the young man – well, he was positively deformed.' A small gesture, 'I couldn't help thinking of *Beauty and the Beast*. Quite unforgivable, of course. But true, I'm afraid.'

The rain, which had been driving against the little window and streaming down the panes, seemed to relent and they took advantage of the lull to get back to the car.

Once there Wycliffe asked, 'On balance, was it worth the trip?'

Lucy said, 'Oh, I think so! A breath of fresh air never did anybody any harm. And I think Mrs Bunt would agree with that. Interesting to know that Morwenna might have a brother or a sister around somewhere. And I can't help wondering about the young man. He shouldn't be difficult to trace.'

'I want to follow up both leads. But first, another word with Miss Rowe at St Ives and the sooner the better.'

Lucy looked at the map. 'From choice I wouldn't start from here, but I expect we shall manage.'

'Hungry?'

'There was a good smell coming from the Bunts' kitchen.'

'We'll eat in St Ives.'

Back at the incident room settling in was complete and things were quiet. The place was beginning to look, feel and smell like home: plastic coffee cups scattered about, the VDUs glowing in blank repose, the phones silent and the radio chattering away comfortably, apparently to itself.

Most of the team were continuing with house-to-house inquiries. Wycliffe, with Lucy Lane, was interviewing the Bunts while Kersey and DC Iris Thorn were left to mind the shop.

For those involved in a police investigation life seems to alternate between phases of frenetic activity and boredom. Kersey was bored, reduced to a crossword in the newspaper. He said, 'Four down: "Apply shellac to see the sweet result". Seven letters – any offers?'

A pause, then Iris Thorn said, 'Try lactose.'

Kersey said, 'I don't get it . . . Yes I do! Iris, you have hidden talents.'

A little later it was, 'Still awake, Iris? Sharpen your wits and try, "O animals become this lady" – eight letters, two words.'

But there was an interruption. A somewhat bedraggled youth entered the hall and stood looking vaguely at the unattended telephones and VDUs. Iris Thorn went to meet him.

'I'm Matthew Mills. I've come about Morwenna.' He looked as though he expected to be arrested on sight.

Kersey called, 'Take him to the interview room, Iris, and stay with him.'

A little later Kersey, who had been briefing himself from the reports, joined the pair with a sheaf of papers which he placed on the table in front of him.

'We've been expecting you to turn up but you've taken your time.'

The boy was about to speak but Kersey cut him short. 'A couple of questions to start: Your full name?'

'Matthew Mills of Ardevera House, St Ives.'

'Aged twenty-two?'

'Yes.'

'Good! So we've got something right. Now it's your turn.'

The lad was very pale and he sat hunched up on his chair, staring down at his feet. He said in a low voice, 'I only heard at lunchtime that Morwenna was dead.'

'But today is Wednesday. Morwenna was fished out of the quarry in her car on Monday afternoon; there was a report on the radio on Monday evening. Yesterday it was on local radio and TV, and in the newspaper. We know you're not living at home at the moment, so where've you been hiding yourself?'

'I've not been hiding; I've got a little motorized caravan and I'm living in that on a caravan park near Constantine. It's called Meadowside.'

'You on full-time holiday or something?'

'No, I work there. I was there last season and they've taken me on again.'

Kersey turned to the wall map. 'Show me where it is on the map.'

Matthew pointed to a woodland area just south of

Constantine village. 'The site adjoins that bit of wood-land.'

Kersey said, 'In this case nowhere is far from anywhere else.' He went on, 'Your mother doesn't seem to know where you are.'

A wan smile. 'Mother would have a fit if she did. She thinks if you've got a degree you should only work in an office or a school or something.'

Kersey shuffled his papers. 'You and Morwenna lived in the same house for several years and later you used to visit her at the hostel near Camborne where she lodged.'

'What? Yes. That's right.'

'Did you fancy her?'

A faint flush on the pale features. 'I was very fond of Morwenna.'

'And you made her pregnant. Did you want to marry her?'

'Yes, but she didn't want that.'

Things were going wrong for Matthew, coming out in the wrong order. He had presented himself ready and anxious to tell everything, now he hardly knew what everything was.

'So Morwenna had an abortion. Were you very upset?'

'Yes.'

'And you held it against her.'

'I just wished she hadn't done it.'

The little room had no window and light came from a low-powered bulb which cast a sickly yellow glow on its dreary starkness. The young man seemed near the end of his tether.

Iris Thorn said, 'What about a coffee break, sir?'

Kersey was about to snap at her but changed his mind. Instead he said to the boy, 'You see? You're the sort women want to cuddle. I wish I was.'

A little later when the coffee cups had been put aside it was Iris Thorn who took over the questioning.

'When did you last see Morwenna?'

It took time to orientate his memory. 'Last Sunday morning.'

Kersey broke in. 'Last Sunday morning. And last Sunday night her car went overboard with her in it.'

There was no response, only a disturbing blankness.

Iris Thorn asked, 'Morwenna knew where to find you?'

'She knew I was working on the site. She'd been to see me several times during the previous couple of weeks and at odd weekends before that.'

Kersey again. 'Are you saying that you knew where she was during the time when everybody was looking for her – including the police?'

'No, I didn't know where she was; she wouldn't tell me. And she made me promise that I wouldn't say that I'd seen her.' His voice was unsteady and he was near to tears. 'She would turn up at odd times. When I happened to come back to the van I would find her just sitting there.'

'Did she come in her Mini?'

'No, she was walking.'

'So it couldn't have been far.'

A helpless gesture. 'She could have left her car anywhere. She wouldn't have wanted it seen on the site. I mean, a yellow Mini . . . Not that anybody would have taken any notice. I mean a caravan site is sort of cut off. They're people on holiday and they don't know or care about anything else.'

Iris Thorn tried again. 'What was she like during these visits? What did she talk about? She must have said something. Did she talk about her illness? We know that she had MS.'

'No, she didn't talk about it but I'm sure she was having trouble. When she walked it wasn't quite right, but she didn't say anything and I didn't dare.'

He stopped, recapturing moments that would always live in his memory. 'Mostly she didn't say much. We drank coffee and sat together. It seemed that she just wanted to make contact, somehow.'

'What about that last visit – on Sunday morning?'

A moment of hesitation then. 'Yes, that was different. She was very disturbed. She said two or three times, "I don't know what I shall do." '

Matthew looked at Iris Thorn. She was not interrogating him like the man; she was encouraging him to offload, and that, as he now realized, was what he most wanted to do.

'She even spoke of going back to St Ives. She said, "I've tried running away from the past and I've tried facing up to it, but neither works." '

'She wouldn't explain, but later she said, "All I've succeeded in doing is to find someone with a bigger problem than my own." '

'Those were her words?'

'I'm not likely to forget them.'

'And with that she left?'

'She said she might not see me for a while but that I wasn't to worry. As she was leaving she said, "Give me time, Matthew. I'll be in touch when I'm ready." '

'So you've no idea where she spent her weekends or the two weeks before she met her death in the quarry. And you didn't try to find out.'

He screwed up his features in his effort to be understood. 'If you knew Morwenna you would realize that there were questions you couldn't ask her.'

'Did you think she was spending time with another man?'

Matthew hesitated before saying very quietly, 'I thought it might be that.'

Kersey looked at the boy as though he were some strange creature from another world. 'And you settled for that?'

A long pause while Kersey made a show of coming to terms with the inexplicable. Then: 'On Monday afternoon didn't you and your caravanners hear all the kerfuffle when the Mini was recovered? It must have made a disturbance for miles around. Didn't you wonder what it was all about?'

Matthew had recovered sufficiently to answer calmly. 'Culdrose Air Station isn't far away and they're always up to something. Nobody takes any notice.'

Kersey studied the youth thoughtfully, before saying, 'For the moment all we want from you is to put what you've told us into a formal statement. Take him away, Iris, and see what you can do with him.'

Wycliffe and Lucy lunched in a little café he knew, close to the new Tate, patronized mainly by locals. It was first names all round and conversations broke out sporadically across the room with no regard for proximity.

The middle-aged waitress seemed to have a natural rapport with everybody and she was bilingual: plain English for visitors, the broad west-Cornish dialect for the rest. 'Do you like grilled mackerel?'

Lucy said, 'I do.'

Wycliffe hesitated. 'It's the bones . . .'

'Use your fingers, dear; nobody minds here.'

He did, with his eye on Lucy, who ended up with a perfect anatomical specimen on her plate, the skeleton devoid of any fragment of flesh.

But he admitted, 'That mackerel was good!'

As Wycliffe and Lucy Lane walked from the restaurant to Ardevera House fat raindrops fell from the leaden sky and thunder rumbled away to the west.

They were admitted by Miss Rowe herself, in her wheelchair. 'Janie's gone shopping but luckily for you I can just manage to open the door for myself.'

A minute or two later they were in the room facing the sea and it started to rain in earnest, lashing against the window so that it was difficult to hear oneself speak. The room was like a sea cave.

'Switch on the lights if you must, but I like it as it is. One of the things I miss most is not being able to go out in what I call "real weather". There, see that!'

A jagged flash cut through the greyness out to sea and was followed at once by a peal of thunder that caused the ornaments on the mantelpiece to rattle.

'Now, Mr Wycliffe, what is this about?'

Wycliffe explained, and Miss Rowe did not disguise her displeasure. Head thrust forward, her arthritic hands gripping the arms of her wheelchair, she demanded, 'What exactly are you asking me?'

'I am asking whether it is true that your sister, Morwenna's mother, had a child by her husband-to-be before they were married?'

Miss Rowe took a moment to consider; then, 'You can rest assured, Mr Wycliffe, that Morwenna was born in wedlock; though I fail to see how the fact can be of concern to you.'

Wycliffe had to wait while another peal of thunder spent itself. 'You have not answered my question, Miss Rowe. I am asking whether there was a child born to the couple before they were married?'

'And if there was?'

'If there was, it follows that Morwenna had a brother or a sister who may well have survived her. I'm told that Morwenna, though possessed of considerable property, died intestate. Those involved in administering the estate would certainly be anxious to contact such a person.'

'And that is your interest? You are not a lawyer.' Miss Rowe was heated.

'No, that is not my interest; I am simply pointing out that inquiries are sure to be made, whether or not I raise the matter.'

Miss Rowe sat back in her chair. 'I see that you have been listening to gossip, though I take your point. I must admit that I did not foresee this difficulty.'

The rain had eased and the sky was lightening. Miss Rowe's spaniel padded into the room and splayed itself at her feet.

Lucy Lane had listened to the exchanges so far without interrupting; now she tried to oil the wheels. 'You see, Miss Rowe, it is the job of the police to find out how and why your niece met her death. Murder is a very real possibility, and we need to know everything that could have a bearing on the inquiry.'

Miss Rowe looked at Lucy, deciding whether to retreat or defend. She retreated.

'All right. I do see that you may need to know these things. At sixteen Bessie did have a child by Barker who, at that time, was a penniless nobody. My parents were very distressed. Bessie was persuaded to have the child in a nursing home and to put it up for adoption at birth.'

Miss Rowe drew in her lips and considered how much further she was prepared to go. 'I have to admit that my attitude was censorious at the time and I was not told any of the details.' She bent over to straighten her skirt as she added, 'I realize that I could have been more supportive of my sister, but I'm afraid that I have always been troubled by the less desirable instincts and prejudices of a born spinster.'

'Do you know the sex of the child?'

'No, I do not. I doubt if Bessie knew herself. It was well managed.'

'Can you tell us the nursing home where the birth took place?'

'My parents saw that she had the very best attention and I have an idea that it was a place in the Truro area. The nursing home was called Saint something.' A faint smile. 'I remember wondering what saints had to do with illegitimate babies.'

'The date of the child's birth?'

Miss Rowe frowned. 'I can only say that it must have been in late July or early August of nineteen sixty-four.'

Wycliffe looked at his watch. 'We were also hoping

for a word with your companion – about her son, Matthew.'

Miss Rowe lifted her bony hands. 'Oh, dear! Poor Janie is so worried. She has not heard from him since before the discovery of Morwenna's body, and she hasn't the least idea where he may be.' She hesitated. 'It would be a kindness if you would make whatever inquiries you think necessary without, at the moment, troubling her. If she hears anything from Matthew she will certainly let you know.'

With that, Wycliffe decided to be content.

Miss Rowe propelled her wheelchair to the front door but they let themselves out into the street.

They were fortunate; the street was running with water but the rain had stopped, and visitors were emerging once more from shops and cafés, looking up at the sky with dubious eyes. The little town had a recurring problem, absorbing, amusing and feeding its guests until the sun shone again.

Wycliffe and Lucy Lane made it to the car-park.

In the car Lucy said, ' "Born out of wedlock," a nice round phrase you rarely hear outside the courts these days. Odd, how quickly the language adapts to changing attitudes.'

Back in his office Wycliffe settled in his chair and listened to Kersey's account of Matthew's visit.

The storm had passed, the air was fresher and watery sunlight filtered through the glass of the little window. Wycliffe said, 'So he's been in touch with the girl, not only while she was missing but at the week-ends before that, yet he still has no idea where she was spending her time.'

'That's his story.'

'You believed him?'

Kersey made one of his baby-frightening grimaces. 'I'd like to say "no" to that, but the boy struck me as such a wet I could believe anything. What puzzles me is how he managed to get her pregnant. She must have drawn diagrams.'

Wycliffe, always irritated by Kersey's apparent obsession with male virility, said, 'Let's leave aside the lad's sexual propensities and talk about the girl's visits to his caravan. In particular about last Sunday morning. I gather she was distressed.'

Kersey grinned. 'My guess is that she thought she'd found a shoulder to cry on but it didn't turn out that way. The boy quoted her. "All I've done is to find someone with a bigger problem than my own." '

Wycliffe was thoughtful. 'It makes one wonder if she committed suicide after all.'

They talked about Morwenna's hypothetical sibling and got nowhere. 'At any rate we must follow that up as well as her apparently casual encounter at the former Barker home mentioned by our Mrs Pearce.'

Then DS Shaw arrived to make his report. In a sense Shaw, like Lister, was a new-model policeman but, unlike Lister, he had little personal ambition. Shaw was only interested in finding a niche where, even in a small way, he could indulge his obsession with that modern pandemic, information technology. At the same time, as a trained accountant, he was the squad's front man in dealing with the breed.

'I've talked to this chap who looks after the girl's business affairs, sir. A real odd-ball. He's keen to tell you that he's not a lawyer and he's not an accountant, but he's handled the Barkers' business affairs ever since George Barker set up in the building trade.

'He's called Swaddling, as in baby bands, and you can't help feeling that he would have been more at home perched on a stool at a high desk writing with a quill pen.'

'So what did he have to say?'

Shaw grinned. 'What didn't he? It took me an hour, but the substance is that Morwenna owned three properties in St Ives and two in the Falmouth area, providing a good income. In addition there is a substantial sum invested mainly in building societies, as her parents left it.'

'So she was a well-off young woman. What did she do with her income?'

'Most of it went into accounts similar to but separate from those held by her parents. In the main, she lived on her earnings.' Shaw grinned. 'I gather Morwenna must have been one of that endangered species who have little interest in money.'

'So who inherits?'

'The old boy says that although he tried many times to persuade Morwenna to go to a lawyer and make a will she consistently put him off.'

'Did he say what he thinks is likely to happen to her estate?'

'Well, after protesting again that he wasn't a lawyer, he said that with no descendants, no sisters or brothers, and no parents or grandparents, the rules of intestacy will probably mean that everything goes to her aunt and her cousin.'

Kersey said, 'Well! There's a turn-up for the book. Our Nicky, a man of property!'

But Wycliffe's thinking was that Morwenna might well have left behind a brother or a sister.

Another report, this time in an envelope from Forensic, on the recovered Mini. It said little and was largely concerned to explain why it couldn't say more. The message seemed to be that a vehicle which has been immersed in water for the better part of twenty-four hours is not the best subject for forensic examination.

In the wake of the storm the sky had cleared, the evening air was fresh, and after a meal Wycliffe went for his walk which, this evening, took him along the seafront. He was late; the sun had set but the sky away to the west was still flushed. The silvery-grey darkened by the minute and the lighthouse beam was beginning to assert itself. A few people paraded, mostly in couples; some were dog-walking.

There were seats, but Wycliffe preferred to stand, arms resting on the wooden rail, staring at the sea. He needed to sort himself out. For one thing he was finding it difficult to maintain a sense of time. It was only six days since Kersey had turned up in his office with the news: that a girl had gone missing. She hadn't been seen for ten days. She worked in a bookshop . . .

But he, Wycliffe, had not become really involved until the discovery of her car in the quarry. When was that? – Monday. Now it was Wednesday.

This case differed from any other that he could remember. Beginning with a missing girl it had led him into a web of relationships between the Barkers, the Bunts and the Meagors. A land deal had gone sour; a man had died, another had gone to prison and killed himself when he came out.

And that man's daughter had set about evening the score – or so it seemed. But she had either killed herself or been killed, and in a spectacular fashion. Assumed to be an only child, it now turned out that she had had an elder brother or sister.

He recalled the former Barker home, the White House that wasn't white, perched on its slope above the valley. He remembered the woman's story of Morwenna's encounter there with a crippled young man . . .

Another thread? Or a quite different strand?

As Wycliffe turned away from his rail he muttered to himself: 'We shall have to see.' A typical conclusion to one of his brooding sessions.

It was almost dark; the wind was freshening and there was more rain in that wind. Wycliffe felt chilled. He walked back at a brisk pace to the hotel and went straight to his room. Once there, he phoned Helen.

'I'm hoping to spend one night at home over the weekend.'

'Things going well?'

'Do they ever?'

'Have a good night anyway, love.'

'You too.'

This was tenderness. Where would he be without it?

Chapter Nine

Thursday 17 August

In the morning there was a stiff south-easterly blowing off the sea and driving curtains of rain inland. When Wycliffe looked out of his bedroom window the air was full of a luminous mist and there were white caps on the waves.

Downstairs the lights were on in the dining room.

Kersey was well into his daily ration of cholesterol while Lucy nibbled her toast and sipped her fruit juice. It was too early for most of the guests on this bleak rainy morning so the police contingent had the dining room almost to themselves.

Half an hour later Wycliffe was in his office, ill-lit and gloomy.

As it happened, for more than an hour he was tied to the telephone in conference with Administration. Weighty matters were discussed: the Economic Utilization of Personnel in the Communications Room; Toilet and Changing Facilities for Female Sergeants; and Parking Facilities at the rear of the Headquarters Building. Considerations remote from the fate of the girl who had suffered from multiple sclerosis and ended her days in a quarry pool.

As Wycliffe listened and put in his pennyworth,

Morwenna, along with the Meagors, the Rowes, the Bunts and the Barkers, receded and was lost in this wider perspective.

For Kersey, the morning was enlivened by the promised visit from Jonathan Meagor.

Another lean, lanky youth. Morwenna's type? He came down the hall, looking about him with obvious nervousness. Kersey was on the platform. Only two of the tables in the hall were occupied; one by Iris Thorn. Jonathan went to her.

Kersey thought, Father's boy.

'I'm Jonathan Meagor. My mother said somebody wanted to talk to me.'

'I do.' Kersey called out from his platform. 'Bring him into the interview room, Iris, and stay with us.'

Kersey had a feeling of *déjà vu*.

Jonathan took his seat across the table from Kersey. Iris Thorn sat in her corner.

'So you've been seeing the dead girl without telling us.' Kersey glared at the boy.

Jonathan looked about the little room as though in search of some way of escape. His voice was tremulous. 'I know that Morwenna is dead . . . I'm very upset about it; but I can't tell you anything about what happened. I just don't know anything.'

'You had your evening meal with her on several nights before she disappeared. You must have talked about something. Didn't she tell you what she was up to with your father? Or what your father was up to with her?'

A deep flush. 'She didn't actually tell me anything.'

'But?'

'She sort of hinted that he wasn't treating her properly.'

'That he was harassing her sexually, is that it?'

'I suppose so.'

'Did you believe her?'

A long pause while Jonathan looked everywhere but at Kersey. 'I found it hard to believe that my father was like that, but why would she make it up?'

'It didn't occur to you that she might be working off a grudge against him because of what had happened to her father?'

'It did occur to me but I didn't want to believe that either.'

A Kersey grin. 'Difficult for you. Did you fancy her?'

'I liked her very much.'

'Ah, that must have been nice. And I suppose she liked you?'

'I don't think so. I was just company.'

'You don't think much of yourself, do you? Who paid?'

'What?'

'Who paid for the meals? Did you? Did she? Or did you go Dutch?'

The boy coloured. 'Morwenna paid. I couldn't have afforded the meals there.'

'Think carefully about this; did she say anything at any time about where she went for those weekends or whether she had a boyfriend – anything like that?'

There was a pause, then, 'One evening when we left the restaurant I tried to . . . well, I tried to be a bit more intimate and she brushed me off.'

'What did she say?'

'Oh, something like, "I've had more than enough of that. I know where it leads." '

'Nothing about her mysterious weekends?'

A longish pause.

'Come on, out with it!'

'It's nothing really, and I don't know whether it had anything to do with where she spent her weekends.'

'But?'

'Well, once she said something about people being odd. I think it was, "You don't know what people are like until you try living with them." And then, "I could never let myself be *dominated*. It's degrading." '

'Was that all?'

'Yes. And when I asked her what she was talking about she said that it was none of my business.'

It seemed that the boy had no more to tell and Kersey said, 'All right; that will do for now but don't get lost; we may need you again.'

When Jonathan had gone, Kersey said, 'A wimp!'

Iris Thorn was indignant. 'Nothing of the kind, sir! A very nice lad. Pity there aren't more like him.'

Kersey yawned. 'Maybe you're right.'

Wycliffe put down the phone and glared at it with malevolence. Not only was he confused, but his ear flaps were sore. He had alternated their use but in vain. At headquarters the top brass had desk microphones.

Returning to earth he began to realize that in the investigation so far he was not following his own recipe. He had not yet got down to exploring the environment of the case. In plainer English, he had made no real effort to get that *feel* for place and people to which he attached so much importance.

Here in Falmouth he was on the sidelines looking in. He might as well have been in his office at headquarters (where his rank would have put him anyway) playing his proper role in the hierarchic paperchase. It was all happening around the Helford River and what he needed was a lead in.

Inspired, he turned to Kersey. 'Jimmy Marsden, a DI in A division. Remember him? I'm pretty sure that when he retired he went back to his roots somewhere in the Constantine area.'

Kersey was engaged in the routine task of digging his nose with a handkerchief and studying with interest what came out. He said, 'I remember Jimmy, and you may be right, but he's probably dead or ga-ga by now.'

Wycliffe was nettled. 'Nonsense! He couldn't have been all that much older than I am.'

Kersey had the sense not to pursue that line. 'All right. I'll get hold of Personnel and find out what happened to him.'

It was a quarter of an hour before Kersey returned. 'They're supposed to be computerized but you'd think they worked out of ledgers written in Chinese.'

'So what did you get?'

'Jimmy was born in nineteen-thirty, so he must be in his middle sixties. He's drawing his pension so he's still with us and, with luck, *compos mentis.*'

'His address.'

'Cherry Tree Cottage, Church Close, Constantine. Sounds like roses round the door.'

'Telephone?'

'I forgot to ask but I'll look him up.'

A few minutes later contact had been made.

'Wycliffe. Remember me?'

'I do indeed, sir.'

Wycliffe explained. 'What about getting together in the pub?'

'No way. I live alone but I don't go without much. If you come here we can talk in comfort.'

So, to Lucy Lane. 'I'm going to Constantine. If I don't ring in I shall be back some time this afternoon.'

Lucy said, 'Do you want me with you?'

'No, I want you to find the sort of up-market nursing home where Morwenna's mother might have had her illegitimate baby – upwards of thirty years ago. Miss Rowe thinks it was in the Truro area and that it was Saint something. Remember the NHS maternity wards are more popular these days and it's likely that some of the private ones will have swopped well-heeled expectant mothers for similarly qualified convalescents or geriatrics.

'Concentrate on the Truro neighbourhood and make a note of any possibles.'

Lucy said, 'Don't forget to take your mobile.'

Constantine has a history going back fourteen centuries, but the present village is largely a product of the granite industry, now defunct. In keeping, the houses on either side of the main street are solid and square and slate-roofed, with no nonsense.

For Wycliffe it was virgin ground. It was absurd! When he left his car on the outskirts of the village and took to walking he felt as though he had made good an escape. It had stopped raining, the wind had dropped and there were patches of blue in the broken sky.

A quarter to twelve.

It wasn't difficult to find the church; and Cherry Tree Cottage, though not within its shadow, was close by in a secluded lane backed by fields.

Detective Inspector Marsden, retired, was in his front garden poking about with a hoe. He was tall, lean and bony and he hadn't changed that much. The path of baldness across the top of his head had broadened, the fringing close-cropped hair had turned grey and he wore spectacles, but he looked weather-tanned and fit.

It took time to dispose of the past but in the end Marsden said, 'When this case blew up I was half expecting a call from Doug Kersey . . . A sad business about the girl. Odd too. It's as if the Barkers had a jinx.'

'You knew the family?'

'In this place everybody knows everybody else – or used to. I was born and brought up in this house and I followed my father's trade as a carpenter until I joined the force at twenty-one. Even then I was posted to Helston after training and I lived mostly at home.' Marsden studied the froth on his tankard. 'What do you think of the brew?'

It was dark and rich, almost creamy. Wycliffe said, 'It's good. Very good!' And meant it.

'My Cherry Tree Special.' Complacent.

Wycliffe felt relaxed and at home. Marsden's living room was a gem. Mantelpiece, dresser, cupboards, table and chairs were of dressed pine. 'All made by my great granddad more than a century ago.'

The floor was of blue slate slabs covered with fibre mats.

'Well, sir, getting back to business . . .'

Wycliffe outlined the case so far. 'At the moment we are after contacts made by the girl during her regular weekends away and during the fortnight she was missing before she was found in the quarry pool.'

'Any leads?'

'Not so's you'd notice. On a day some time during this past winter she was seen around her former home in conversation with a youngish man. According to our witness he was badly deformed though he got around well enough with the help of a stick—'

Wycliffe broke off. 'You were going to say something?'

'Yes, a name comes to mind though I suppose it's a long shot. A young chap called Cross. He's a cripple. Born like it, they say. He lives in a biggish house by the creek at Polwheveral with his mother, a retired doctor.'

Marsden looked at Wycliffe over his spectacles. 'Doesn't all that ring a bell?'

'Should it?'

'You don't remember the case. It was some years ago. The boy's father, another doctor – a psychiatrist, I believe, took himself off one morning on his regular walk and just vanished off the face of the earth. I don't suppose you were directly involved but you would have seen the reports.'

Marsden took a gulp of his beer and wiped his lips. 'It was Tom Reed's case but I remember it because of the local connection and the fact that I knew the people.'

'And the son still lives with his mother in this house on the creek?'

'Ventonbos. It's buried amongst the trees on the west side.'

'They live alone?'

'There's a housekeeper or companion, whatever you like to call her.' Marsden made a vague gesture. 'It's an odd set-up. They're hardly ever seen in the village and it surprises me that the son, if it was him, was on the loose with the girl.'

Wycliffe said, 'I think I'll pay a little visit.'

Marsden grinned. 'You haven't changed, sir. Still no use for protocol. You've got your car?'

'Yes, but I'll walk.'

'That figures. In that case I'll show you on the map.'

On the map, just south of the village, there was a footpath to Polwheveral through what seemed to be a wooded valley.

'Very pretty,' Marsden said. 'Of course they've built a sewage works down there but you can't smell it and you can look the other way, so it's not too bad.'

Wycliffe got up to go but Marsden detained him. 'You may have noticed a nice smell coming from the kitchen – Marsden's *potage suprême*. It's one o'clock, there's plenty of it, so if you care to join me . . .'

The footpath to Polwheveral was criss-crossed by tree roots and subject to abrupt changes in level, but the trees were in full leaf, the sun was shining, the gulls were flying high and it was pleasantly cool. He could hear but not see the stream and he missed the sewage works altogether.

In less than half a mile he arrived for the first time in Polwheveral.

A memorable first.

A few houses of varied provenance on a country lane. On the other side of the lane, a hedge, and one or two buildings separated the hamlet from the creek proper. Wycliffe found his way there through what appeared to be the backyard of a gaunt, mill-like building on to an expanse of waterlogged spongy grass intersected by narrow channels. Here and there the slender mast of some small craft pointed skyward. Clear water shone in the distance, and on either side woodland almost embraced the creek.

The silence was absolute. He retraced his steps to the hamlet. A dog found him, but it was a while before he found a human being, a man tinkering with a lawnmower in his garden.

'Ventonbos?' A moment of hesitation, then the man pointed to the west side of the creek. 'It's among the trees over there. Follow the road and you'll find a track off to your left.'

Wycliffe found the track and followed it under arching trees until it ended in the backyard of a substantial house, four-square, hip-roofed, and with a round dozen of chimney pots. Ventonbos was typical of many small estates carved out of the countryside for the growing class of prosperous mine owners and managers in the early eighteen-hundreds.

An ageing Escort was parked near the house. A man, slashing away at encroaching brambles on rising ground above the yard, called out, 'You want something, mister?'

'I'm looking for Dr Cross.'

Another double take then, 'You'd best go round the front.' He pointed with his pruning hook.

In front of the house only a weedy paved terrace separated it from encroaching nettles, brambles and sapling trees. The main body of the woodland sloped steeply to the creek, seemingly impenetrable, but Wycliffe could just glimpse its waters through the trees.

Once more the silence asserted itself, an entity that was almost palpable. Wycliffe found himself listening to it.

The front door of the house stood open to a hall paved with honey-coloured stone and an attractive cantilevered staircase added a touch of elegance. There was no bell, no knocker, so he rapped on the door with his knuckles.

Marsden had mentioned a housekeeper or companion and the words had conjured up for Wycliffe a long, lean, grey dragon. His vision had to undergo rapid revision. The woman who answered his knock was in her early thirties (much too young to be the doctor herself), pleasant to look at, with fair hair to her shoulders. She wore a very short, plain blue dress exposing a lot of plump thigh. There was something distinctly adolescent about her, and the pearls around her neck seemed oddly inappropriate, like a schoolgirl dressing up.

'Detective Superintendent Wycliffe. I wish to speak to Dr Florence Cross.'

A mere glance at his warrant card; no fluster, no hint of police phobia. 'I'm Isobel Wilde; I live with Dr Cross. If you will come inside, please, I'll get her.'

He was shown into a large room on the left of the hall: a sitting room, a study, a library. There were books everywhere including heaps on the floor. A table by the window was littered with papers, and on another, by the fireplace, there was a word processor; more papers and more books. A grand piano in one corner had been treated with unique respect: no clutter on its lid.

In this room it was obvious that tidiness came well down the list of priorities and a visiting vacuum cleaner would have to tackle virgin ground. But the overall effect of barely controlled slovenliness was not without its appeal for Wycliffe.

Perhaps the most striking single object in the room was a painting over the fireplace: a portrait of a young woman seated and in profile. Her pale, strictly defined features and straight blonde hair, in page-boy style, had the effect of a cut-out set against the sombre *mélange* of blues and browns which formed the background of the painting.

'Superintendent Wycliffe? . . . Florence Cross.'

He turned to confront the original. The sitter had aged, of course; the pale, acutely defined features were sharper still, and the straight blonde hair was being assisted in the preservation of its colour and sheen. Tight tartan trousers covered long thin legs and she wore a black velvet waistcoat over a white shirt. The overall impression was still one of a vigorous woman in later middle life.

Dr Florence was followed closely by her companion.

'Now, how can we help you?' Wycliffe was given an armchair on one side of the fireplace while the two women seated themselves on a settee opposite. Isobel sat knees together, her dress pulled down as far as it would go.

Wycliffe decided on caution. 'I am investigating the death of a young woman, Morwenna Barker—'

'Morwenna? Did you say her *death*? Are you saying that Morwenna is *dead*?' A shocked interruption.

'I'm afraid so.'

'But she was here with us last week. She only left on Sunday . . .' Dr Florence turned to her companion. 'Isobel! do you hear that?'

Isobel rested a consoling hand on the other's arm. 'I can't believe it!'

Wycliffe felt reassured to the extent that he had come to the right place. So far, so good. He went on, matter-of-fact in voice and manner. 'On Monday Morwenna Barker's body was discovered in her car, in several feet of water, at the bottom of the quarry known as Job's Pit. The pathologist says that she had been in the water for less than twenty-four hours.'

Dr Florence leaned forward, her pale features strained, her whole manner expressive of incredulity. 'It's not possible!'

'Are you saying that you knew nothing of this, Dr Cross? . . . Miss Wilde? . . .' Wycliffe looked from one to the other. 'There was a report of the discovery on the radio on Monday evening. It is now Thursday. In the meantime there have been further reports in the papers, on the radio and on television.'

It was Isobel who spoke. 'You must understand, superintendent, that we are trying to come to terms with what you have just told us. As to our not knowing, I suppose that our way of going on is unusual. We have no television, we use the radio mainly for music and we take a newspaper only on

Sundays.' A firm come-back. Perhaps there was more to Isobel than met the eye.

The doctor was silent, staring into the empty grate.

It was either genuine, or a good act. They were believable. People who choose to isolate themselves in the back of beyond were hardly likely to be devotees of the media news circus.

But Wycliffe had to get his facts straight. 'For some months Morwenna spent her weekends away from the shop and the flat where she lived and worked. Did she spend them here?'

'Yes. It was no secret as far as we were concerned, but she wanted it that way.'

'And the fortnight before her body was discovered in the quarry?'

'Yes. As I told you, she left on Sunday. Again, it was her wish that no-one should know that she was here.'

Outside the sky had clouded over and the misty rain had returned. Wycliffe sat, looking like anything but a policeman. People saw him as a mild-mannered man; patient, with a ready sympathy. People wondered if that was the real Wycliffe, and sometimes he wondered himself.

Dr Florence found words. 'You say that Morwenna and her car were recovered from Job's Pit? That's not much more than a mile from here.' She broke off. Then, 'It's hard to believe . . . I assume that she took her own life? I mean, it could hardly have been an accident.'

Wycliffe was vague. 'We are looking into possibilities. Would it surprise you if it turned out to be suicide?'

The doctor shook her head. 'I don't know. I really don't know what to say or even think. Morwenna was certainly not a happy young woman. She had little reason to be.'

She turned to her companion. 'What do you think, Isobel?' But Isobel responded with no more than a vague gesture, and Dr Florence continued, 'I assume that you must know by now that she suffered from multiple sclerosis?

'Add to that her distress and bitterness concerning what had happened to her family. All, in consequence, she believed, of perjury on the part of that bookseller – Meagor, I think his name is.'

She looked up. 'I imagine that none of this is news to you?'

Wycliffe did not answer directly. 'I understand that she had the idea of punishing Mr Meagor by going to work in his shop, sharing his flat, and using her position to undermine him.'

A quick nod. 'Yes, that is so, unfortunately. We did what we could to dissuade her but Morwenna is – was – a very determined young woman. I could understand her bitterness but it was obvious that in the long run she would achieve very little and might only do herself harm.'

Dr Florence contemplated her pale, slender hands. 'This is deeply distressing . . . I can't come to terms with it, and I feel that we are in some way responsible.'

Wycliffe regretted having come alone. Accompanied by a DC you cannot be mistaken for anything but what you are, but this visit was taking on aspects of a social call.

He decided on a spot of formality through direct

questions. 'Was it through your son, Dr Cross, that Morwenna was introduced into this house?'

'What?' The doctor looked up abruptly. 'Oh yes. It was. Julian met her by chance. I was so pleased. I was beginning to despair of him ever having the company of someone nearer his own age. And Morwenna was such a lovely girl. Now . . .'

He tried to catch her off balance. 'I understand that your husband left home some time ago.'

Its apparent irrelevance gave the remark an edge, but it took her only a moment to re-orientate and without obvious resentment. 'Yes. Actually it was five years ago last February. That, of course, was a very great shock. Raymond went off for his usual morning walk and never came back.

'His papers and books on the table by the window are just as he left them.' She glanced around the room and went on, 'In fact, very little has changed here since he went.'

She looked at Wycliffe as though in doubt. 'It's quite silly, mere superstition, of course, but I have the feeling that as long as his things remain undisturbed there is a chance that he will come back.'

A brief pause and she added, 'He was actually working on the second volume of his book, preparing it for the press when he went.'

'His book?'

'*The Psychology of Deformity.* Raymond was quite a notable figure in his profession and he contributed regularly to the journals.'

She was becoming almost garrulous and Wycliffe chose this time to push her a little further. 'I would like to talk to your son.'

She looked surprised. 'Really? If you think it's necessary. He's in his workroom.' She turned to her companion. 'Isobel, would you mind? You will have to break it to him, dear; he will take it better from you.'

Isobel said, 'Of course.'

Wycliffe stood up. 'I'll come with you if I may.'

Isobel turned back from the door. 'But I wanted to break the news to him alone. He will be very distressed.'

Wycliffe was firm. 'Dr Cross, Miss Wilde, it is only fair to tell you that Morwenna may have been murdered.'

Consternation. 'You are saying that someone might have murdered her? But that's not possible! Who would—'

Wycliffe was patient. 'As I say, murder is a possibility, and since coming here this afternoon I've learnt that this is where she spent her weekends as well as the two weeks preceding her death. In the circumstances you must see that both of you and Mr Cross could be important witnesses. No more and no less.'

A moment for reflection then the doctor said, 'This is a nightmare!'

Wycliffe was puzzled. All the reactions of the two women seemed to lie within that broad spectrum that is called normality, and yet he had the uncomfortable feeling that he was being taken for a ride.

Isobel said, 'All right, Mr Wycliffe. If you must. This way.' She added, 'Julian is a naturalist, principally interested in flies. As you will see, his room is a sort of laboratory. Please remember that he is a very sensitive young man.'

Wycliffe followed her down a gloomy passage, past

the kitchen, to a small room at the back of the house. The door was open. There were shelves with books and bottles, a cabinet of glass-topped shallow drawers and a pervasive, not unpleasant, smell of ether. A man, a bulky figure, sat at a bench by the window studying something through a binocular microscope. On the bench beside the microscope one of the shallow drawers, its glass top removed, held flies pinned out in rows, each carrying its tiny label.

Isobel said, 'Julian, this is Superintendent Wycliffe, he wants to talk to you.'

The man pushed back his chair, got heavily to his feet, and turned to face them.

'Mr Wycliffe, this is Dr Cross's son, Julian.'

Julian's body was ungainly and lop-sided. His head, which seemed large in relation to his body, was held at an angle. His features were pale and his hair seemed altogether lacking in pigment.

Isobel went on, 'He's brought some very sad news, Julian. About Morwenna.'

Wycliffe said his piece and the young man listened without apparent emotion, but then he said, 'I'm afraid I must sit down.'

Back in his chair he pushed away the microscope. 'You are saying that she killed herself?' His voice had a pleasant timbre; he spoke slowly, and his manner was subdued.

'We are investigating her death.'

'What does that mean?' The question came sharply.

'We are investigating the possibility of murder.'

'I see.' Wycliffe was at a loss to read the expression in the intensely blue eyes.

'When did you last see Morwenna?'

'What? Oh, on Sunday.'

'The day she left.'

'I suppose so – yes.' There was a strange hesitancy about his replies as though his thoughts were running on lines that were cut across by these questions.

When the three of them returned to the sitting room, Dr Florence looked anxiously at her son, 'You must try to understand, Julian.' Though she did not say what it was that he should understand.

Wycliffe resorted to routine. 'Later you will be asked, each of you, to come to the police station to make formal statements concerning Morwenna's stay here and the circumstances in which she left. You will have plenty of notice and, of course, transport will be provided.'

The doctor said, 'Shall we be involved in any other way?'

'I'm afraid so. This is where Morwenna spent much of the time leading up to her death and I can't emphasize too strongly our need to know everything possible about her and her relationships. All I can say is that we shall cause as little inconvenience as possible.'

'Obviously you must do what you think necessary.'

'Yes, and I want you to be quite clear about the position. Morwenna's body was recovered on Monday afternoon. The pathologist is of the opinion that she had been in the water less than twenty-four hours, and that she died shortly before immersion. Almost certainly at some time on Sunday night.'

Wycliffe shifted in his chair. 'Now. You tell me that she left here on Sunday. At what time?'

The two women looked at each other and Isobel

said, 'It must have been between nine and ten in the morning.'

'Can you tell me how she was dressed?'

A pause for consideration before Dr Florence said, 'She was wearing a green overshirt with matching trousers. She was very fond of green.'

'No coat?'

Hesitation. 'She wasn't wearing one but she might have had a light raincoat or something over her arm.'

Isobel said, 'Yes, she did. I remember.'

'Did she say where or why she was going? Did she say whether or when she would be back?'

Dr Florence frowned. 'It wasn't quite like that. Morwenna was free to come and go as she felt inclined. I think that was one of the reasons why she came to us. She knew that she wouldn't be questioned or tied in any way . . .'

'So she left here between nine and ten on Sunday morning and, according to the pathologist, she died less than twenty-four hours later.'

Dr Florence chose not to comment and Wycliffe seemed in no hurry to continue. There was an awkward silence.

In the gloom colours were muted and their faces stood out, abnormally pale.

Wycliffe spoke at last. 'I should tell you that there is evidence to suggest that Morwenna might have been injured, carried in a semi-conscious condition to her car, and then driven to the quarry.'

The nasty medicine at last, served without jam.

Dr Florence whispered, 'Oh, my God!' Then, 'What you say is terrible, but I must insist that we know nothing of what happened to the poor girl after she left here on Sunday morning.'

Isobel nodded.

Through all this Julian had been sitting, hands on knees, staring straight in front. He said nothing and his features displayed no discernible emotion.

Wycliffe himself was having difficulty in getting the situation into perspective. It had developed almost out of the blue; starting with Mrs Pearce, erstwhile neighbour of the Barkers, referring to a casual encounter she had witnessed between Morwenna and a crippled young man.

The crippled young man had brought him, via Marsden, to Ventonbos, on what seemed no more than a fishing trip. But Ventonbos had turned out to be Morwenna's refuge during those mysterious weekends, as well as for the last two weeks of her life.

It was not the first time that his unorthodox behaviour had landed him in a tricky situation. Having shown his hand to vital witnesses he was having to walk away allowing them, if they wanted or needed to, the chance to collude and present a united front.

But if they were guilty of anything wouldn't they have done that already? He salved his conscience. 'Before leaving I would like to see the room Morwenna had while she was here.'

Dr Cross once more enlisted her companion. 'Would you, Isobel? Do you mind?'

Isobel, subdued but co-operative, led him to a small room at the front of the house. It was ordinary: a single bed, chest of drawers, dressing table and wardrobe, all fifties style.

'I slept here when I first came to Ventonbos.'

'And when was that?'

'Oh, fifteen or sixteen years ago.'

So Isobel would have been in her late teens when she arrived at Ventonbos. (Was Morwenna a potential successor?) And for ten years after Isobel's arrival Dr Raymond Cross, husband and consultant psychiatrist, would have still been around.

As a matter of form, Wycliffe looked in the wardrobe and opened drawers at random. 'She left some of her things here.'

'Of course; she expected to be back and we assumed that she would be.'

Wycliffe was trying to order in his mind the flood of new information and to get some feeling for the people involved.

Dr Raymond Cross, no longer present; Dr Florence Cross; the crippled Julian; Isobel Wilde; and, finally, Morwenna Barker, deceased.

Julian with his deformity and his flies.

Wycliffe stood by the bed, pondering. Perhaps Isobel misunderstood, for she said, 'I don't know what is in your mind, Mr Wycliffe, but there was no question of sex between Julian and Morwenna. They were both looking for companionship, no more than that.'

She seemed to make the point with some force.

There were questions to be asked – many, but now was not the time.

They went back downstairs and Wycliffe prepared to leave. Standing in the hall with Dr Florence, at the open door and looking towards the creek, he said, 'How long have you lived here?'

'More than thirty years.'

'Do you go away much?'

'Since I retired from the practice I hardly ever leave here. For one thing, I gave up driving after an accident, and I'm dependent on Isobel for everything.'

Wycliffe said, 'Well, you live in a very beautiful place.'

'But?' She was quick to sense his reservation.

'It's also a very strange place.'

She nodded. 'Yes. Sometimes I think it has possessed us.'

Wycliffe left. He walked back through the valley and up through the village to where he had parked his car. It was raining; fine rain that was little more than a mist. He decided that at least he had found somewhere to start. Also that, in this instance, speed was not of the essence.

Let them stew. He needed to know more of their background, a great deal more. And when the time came to move in it would have to be a well-thought out and discreet operation. No heavy stuff. Atmosphere was at least as important as material evidence.

Chapter Ten

Wycliffe was back in his office. Suddenly the case had opened up and he was having to make choices about which line to follow first. The Cross family – family was the wrong word. The Cross ménage. That was better. Wycliffe attached importance to words. He had discovered that without realizing it horizons can be narrowed or expanded by the choice of a word.

Both the missing Raymond and his wife Florence were doctors, and doctors meant Franks; a veritable compendium of gossip about colleagues, past and present. Wycliffe telephoned and was lucky to find the pathologist in his office.

Wycliffe explained.

'I could tell as soon as I picked up the phone, Charles, that you wanted something. Can't you get hold of a medical register?'

'What would it tell me of any use? About you, for example?'

Franks chuckled. 'As I thought, it's dirt you're after. I wonder what would happen if I started quizzing you about bent coppers. Anyway, what poor devil is it this time? What's he supposed to have done? And do I know him?'

'There are two of them, Dr Raymond and Dr Florence Cross, husband and wife – at least they were, I believe. I don't know that either of them have done anything to upset us. I'm after background.'

Franks began to sound interested. 'Ah! I have come across the lady; a consultant obstetrician. She may not have upset you, but a few years back she managed to upset the GMC.'

'She wasn't struck off?'

'No, as I remember, she got away with a slapped wrist. Something about lesbian frolics with a couple of her patients. I don't know the details but I suppose I could ferret 'em out if I have to. Anyway she must be into her sixties by now and she's probably given up bedroom sports.'

'And the man?'

'I know that he was a psychiatrist and that he wrote a book on the subject – Dr Raymond Cross, that was it. Out of my line. I think he went ga-ga and did away with himself. Something like that. I'm not surprised, I keep away from that sort of thing for fear of catching it.'

Franks added, 'You're on to a funny family, Charles.'

Wycliffe said his thanks and put down the phone, only to sit staring at it as though it were some sort of icon from which inspiration might be expected. Perhaps it worked, for he muttered, 'So she was an obstetrician. Could it be . . . ? That would be too far-fetched.'

But the thought lingered; to surface again later.

Marsden had said that Tom Reed dealt with the Cross disappearance. That at least was a line easily followed.

But Kersey came in. 'I gather you've had fun, sir.'

'If that's what you call it, but never mind that now. Cross – Dr Raymond Cross – does the name ring a bell?'

Kersey's wrinkles deepened. 'I've got a feeling it should . . . It goes back a few years. He was the chap who walked out on his family and disappeared off the face of the earth. At least that's what they said. It was Tom Reed's case.'

Wycliffe was puzzled. 'It's odd, but I don't remember a thing about it.'

Kersey nodded. 'I'm not surprised. You were on sick leave; flu followed by pleurisy. You'll remember that. Anyway, I'll get them to dig out the file.'

'And I'll have a word with Tom.'

Again he was lucky to catch the retired DI at the end of a phone. Friendly courtesies exchanged – and it was good to hear the old fog-horn bellow once more – they got down to business.

'Raymond Cross? Yes, I remember that case well – must have been about five years back. Man and wife, both doctors. According to her, Raymond had gone a bit queer in the head; given to wandering off. And one day he wandered off and didn't come back. That was her story and she stuck to it. Her son backed her up and so did the woman who lived with them.'

Tom heaved a great sigh before adding, 'That was where we started and that was where we finished. After searching the whole area: creeks, cliffs, quarries and God knows what; and questioning the populace for miles around, into the bargain.'

'Your thoughts?'

'I was afraid you were going to ask me that. The

Cross woman struck me as odd, but so did the whole bloody set-up. I mean, their house at the head of that creek . . . Lovely place and all that, but it would've driven me round the twist to live there with those two women. And the old boy had a head start, he was a psychiatrist.'

'But?'

'What can I say? When three key witnesses tell the same story, and stick to it, there's not much a poor copper can do. As you know, sir, the rack isn't popular with the CPS. Anyway, what's happened now?'

'The girl who went over with her car into a quarry pool was staying, almost living, there.'

Reed was impressed. 'Well, there's a turn-up for the book! I don't envy you having to cope with that trio.'

Wycliffe dropped the phone and turned to Kersey. 'I think we'd better have that file.'

It was early evening; the others had gone back to the hotel for their meal. 'Tell them I shan't be in for dinner.'

He was still in his office. It was cloudy and the light was failing, but he had not bothered to switch on his lamp. He sat brooding. He no longer doubted that Morwenna had been murdered and he was convinced that her death was linked to her stay at Ventonbos.

He was troubled by what he had learned of Morwenna's last day. At Ventonbos they claimed that she had left for the last time on Sunday morning.

According to the medical evidence she was alive shortly before her car went over the quarry edge at some time on Sunday night.

Matthew Mills had said that she was with him in his caravan for a time on Sunday morning.

There were missing hours.

He got up from his chair, moving stiffly; the gloomy box-like room seemed chilly and there were streaks of rain on the window.

Usually, when he was away from home on a case he established some sort of routine – where he had his meals, the pubs he visited, the extent and nature of those evening walks.

But not this time. Once more he had to remind himself that he was dealing with events so recent that there had been no time to create any sort of routine.

Anyway, he decided he would set going some sort of routine by having his meal at Martha and Mary's in the High Street.

The little restaurant looked cosily full but Martha found him a table. She must have made some reassessment of the superintendent; she was positively genial. 'You're in luck tonight, Mr Wycliffe. It's roast chicken with tarragon in a white wine sauce, little boiled potatoes tossed in butter and tender runner beans. That with a chilled lager or a glass of Chablis, and you won't do better.'

Afterwards he walked aimlessly through the fine drizzle and at last found himself back in Moor Street, outside the bookshop. The premises were in darkness; no light even from the dormer window.

For once he felt in need of company and the pub opposite looked inviting.

They made room for him at the bar and there was an awkward lull while he was served with his lager. He took it to one of the marble-topped tables by a window away from the bar and soon the decibel output was restored.

A moment or two, a couple of sips, and he was aware of being watched by one of the men still at the bar; a young man, painfully thin, his pale features framed dramatically by his black hair.

Nicky Barker. They had never met but Kersey's description left no room for doubt.

It wasn't long before Barker came to his table, glass in hand, his manner subdued, tentative. 'I'm Nicky Barker. I would like a word.'

Wycliffe said nothing.

Barker sat down. 'You probably know about me already and your DI will fill in any gaps.'

With his finger Barker drew a circle in spilled beer on the table top. 'I've got to admit, I'm knocked sideways by what happened to Wenna.' He raised his eyes to meet Wycliffe's. 'Think of it; I'm only in my twenties and I've nobody left – no relatives close enough to call relatives. It's a funny feeling.'

'So?'

'I want to get to the bottom of this. Did Wenna kill herself? If not, who killed her? You think she was murdered, otherwise you wouldn't be down here for a start.'

Barker was speaking in low tones with an urgency that was compelling and Wycliffe took him seriously. 'You must realize that we are asking the same questions.'

'Sure, but . . .' He broke off, finished his beer and put down his glass. 'It seems to me that what happened to her father sort of triggered all this off.' A long pause, then, 'She thought he was stitched-up for clocking Roach. If she'd known the truth things might have been different.'

'The truth?'

'I could have told her. He was guilty all right. For once your lot got the right man.'

Wycliffe said nothing and after a while Barker took up where he had left off. 'I was still living with them then and I remember that night. I'm not likely to forget it. The old man came home about three in the morning. I was in bed but awake. It was pissing down with rain . . . Aunt Bessie was waiting up for him . . .

'I went to the top of the stairs and listened. He'd walked home. Eight bloody miles in that downpour. He must've bin like a drowned rat. Aunt Bessie fussed, but he shut her up. "I've killed a man . . ." '

Wycliffe had a vivid picture in his mind of Chygwyn, the little house on the slope, buffeted by the wind and swept by the rain. The youth on the landing, leaning over the banisters, listening, determined to know what was going on in a family where his presence was no more than tolerated.

Another aspect to the evolution of a toe-rag.

Barker stopped speaking; he fiddled with his empty glass, and Wycliffe waited.

'They began to talk in whispers and I couldn't hear a thing. I went back to bed. I was going to stay awake until they came upstairs; their bedroom was next to mine. But I fell asleep, and next thing I knew it was morning.'

It was obvious that this bizarre young man, with his lank hair and frilly black blouse, was reliving a cardinal incident in his life.

He took a deep breath. 'When I went downstairs in

the morning I couldn't believe it . . . Aunt Bessie was a bloody marvel! I mean, it was like nothing had happened! The old man had gone off to work and she was sitting down with her cup of bloody tea! And Wenna was having her breakfast before going to school . . .'

'Morwenna knew nothing?'

'She must have slept through it. More's the pity, as it turned out.'

'But later, when she started her campaign against Meagor, you never thought to put her straight. In fact you took money from her for helping her out.'

Barker shrugged. 'She was serious, but it was no more than a lark as far as I was concerned – and an opportunity to make a few quid. I don't deny that. The way I live you can't pass up a chance, but I never realized what it would lead to. I'm asking, do you think it could have had anything to do with Wenna ending up in the quarry?'

'I can't answer that, but I shall think over what you have told me and it may be necessary for you to make a statement.'

Barker sat back on his chair, 'Well, at least you've listened. And that's something, from any copper.'

Wycliffe stood up. As a conversation in a pub with a senior police officer this had got out of hand. Time to put the stopper in. 'You've admitted to being involved in criminal harassment and you would be well advised to watch your step in future. Don't get lost. As I said, we may need you.'

One of the oddest encounters Wycliffe had known in a long career. He walked back to the hotel, wondering.

Was Nicky to be taken seriously? And if so, did it change anything? Not now. He was merely saying that the courts had got it right. But if Morwenna had *known* that her father was a guilty man would she still have set up her hate campaign against Meagor? If not, her future, and that of others, might have been very different.

But start looking for first causes and you're back to the Big Bang or Adam in the Garden. According to taste.

Before going to bed he phoned Helen, then he stood looking out of his window at the smooth dark sea and at the slow measured blinking of St Anthony's light. Soothing subjects for contemplation, both of them.

But in bed he could not get Nicky Barker's story out of his mind. What was the young man's motive in speaking now? Some belated attempt at restitution? Even after thirty-odd years in the force Wycliffe still liked to believe that no-one is wholly bad.

Friday 18 August

Another day of broken cloud but the wind had dropped and there was the promise of a warm day. At breakfast Wycliffe broke the news to Kersey.

'You believe anything that comes from that toe-rag, sir? You can see what he's up to. Clean the slate a bit then perhaps he'll be in with a better chance when the pay-out comes.'

Wycliffe was curt. 'His story, as far as Barker is concerned, merely confirms the court's findings, but he may be useful as the case develops.'

In the incident room the programme for the day was worked out. Lucy had done her homework on nursing/ maternity homes. 'There was just one top-of-the-market establishment in the Truro district which had specialized in maternity cases. It was called St Agatha's; now it's switched to well-heeled convalescents and changed its name to the Tresillian Nursing Home – and that's where it is – Tresillian, about three miles out of Truro.'

They drove there. Lucy said, 'The plot thickens.'

The Tresillian Nursing Home occupied a large Victorian house in its own grounds overlooking the Tresillian River. The gravelled drive and broad green lawns were bordered by shrubs and backed by trees. A couple of Volvos, a bullish-looking Daihatsu and a BMW waited on the gravel, exposed to the weather. In the heated glassed-in porch, two female convalescents, silver hair meticulously waved, were laid out on boat-deck chairs, chatting amiably, exchanging their dietary and medical titbits.

Lucy said, 'I don't like these places.'

They were received by an efficient young secretary. 'The manageress? Oh, you mean the director. May I ask your business?' Then, 'Oh, police. If you'll wait just a moment.'

They were shown into a white, sanitized office to meet a woman in her fifties; plump and faultlessly dressed in a white blouse and grey two-piece. Her manner had something of the kindly bossiness of that extinct species, the hospital matron.

Wycliffe opened negotiations: 'I'm inquiring about something that happened just over thirty years ago, in nineteen sixty-four. At that time I believe you specialized in maternity cases. I wonder if you can help me?'

A cautious response. 'Perhaps. I came here in fifty-eight.' A faint smile. 'Of course I wasn't in charge then.'

'In July or August of nineteen sixty-four a baby was born to a sixteen-year-old girl called Elizabeth or Bessie Barker.'

'I'm afraid I can't give you information about individual patients.'

'But you have records dating back that far?'

'Of course.'

'We are investigating a possible murder and we could obtain a court order, but that would be time-consuming and the information I need is unlikely to harm anyone.'

'I will help you where I can.'

'Presumably a doctor would have attended the birth.'

'Naturally.'

'Could you let me have the name of that doctor?'

'I think that should be possible.'

She was gone some time and when she came back she had with her a slim, ledger-like book which she leafed through. 'Ah, here we are! . . . I remember that case. I was a junior nurse in the delivery room.' A dreamy look in the blue eyes. 'It was a difficult birth, in fact a difficult pregnancy, and a consultant obstetrician was brought in.'

'Do you have the name of that consultant?'

'Of course. It was a Dr Florence Cross; a remarkable woman. At that time she was still in her early thirties but well known and highly respected. She became quite a regular here until the nature of our work changed.'

Wycliffe felt that the gods were on his side.

'I believe that the baby was adopted at birth?'

'Yes, but I am not able to give you any information on that score without other authority.'

'Will you tell me the date of birth?'

'July the thirty-first.'

'And the sex of the child?'

'It was a boy; and I'm afraid that is all I can tell you.'

Wycliffe decided not to push his luck. He thanked her and they were shown out.

Back in the car Lucy said, 'Dr Florence Cross; a boy child adopted at birth . . .'

'You're reading my thoughts, Lucy.'

'Really, sir? And I thought I was having some of my own.'

Lucy was concentrating on the twists and turns in the narrow lane leading back to the main road.

Wycliffe said, 'At least we're in a position to ask a few very pertinent questions.'

Back in the incident room, on Wycliffe's table, there was a slender file from Missing Persons: 'Raymond Bassett Cross, MB; B.Ch.; FRCPsy. Age: 59. Missing from his home since, approximately, 06.30 hours, 20th February.'

There followed a description of the man: 'One metre fifty-six; slight build; tanned skin; fair hair, turning grey and thinning, clipped moustache; blue eyes. Wearing grey pin-striped suit with matching cap, light raincoat and walking boots.'

'Informant: Dr Florence Cross of same address. Wife.'

The only photograph available portrayed a younger man. Late forties? Lean, wiry, intense; eyes staring at the camera with a hint of aggression, as though resentful of the intrusion.

Wycliffe scanned the notes.

Dr Cross was in the habit of taking long walks in the early morning. His choice of route, unpredictable. Anywhere within a radius of five or six miles. According to reports from interviews with villagers, some years before his disappearance Cross had changed. From a busy professional man, respected if not liked, he had become morose, eccentric and reclusive. A similar story came from the hospital where Cross had resigned his consultancy and ceased to have anything to do with his former colleagues.

Missing Persons routine had been followed: some questioning of neighbours and acquaintances; inquiries among taxi and car-hire firms; a fruitless search along the shores and among the quarries with a helicopter flight or two over the same ground.

Wycliffe could guess the conclusion from all this: suicide/accident; the former more probable. The body would turn up somewhere, sometime. Meanwhile not much more would or could be done about it.

Wycliffe's imagination was easily stirred by the thought of someone who walks out of his/her home on some quite ordinary errand and is never seen or heard of again. It's rare, but it happens. Every police force in the country could attest to that.

He tried to visualize the doctor striding off in his grey pin-striped suit and matching cap, probably carrying a stick. A slim, dapper figure, trim moustache, bronzed skin, and an air of self-conscious importance. Only to disappear off the face of the earth.

Wycliffe smiled at his own fancy.

The triumvirate lunched in the little restaurant which was part of the old town hall building. They had a table in an alcove where they could talk.

'So, we move in. If you will look after the shop, Doug, I'll take Lucy and a DC. The question is which? Any ideas, Lucy?'

'My choice would be Iris Thorn, sir.'

'Another woman. Might be a good idea.'

Over the years Wycliffe had conquered a prejudice which he had never once acknowledged – women in the force. Now he was working from choice with two of them.

Kersey said, 'Shouldn't Fox be in on this?'

Wycliffe was decisive. 'No, I want an interpretation, not an inventory.' He sat back in his chair. 'So that's settled. And the watchword is a light touch. We want to see that place and those people from the inside without the kind of aggro that might set them thinking about lawyers.'

After lunch, a briefing, for what Kersey insisted on calling the 'boarding party'.

On Wycliffe's first visit to Ventonbos he had been alone and regretted it. Now he was going with support and much better briefed as to background, but if he followed the book he would have been bringing these people in for formal interviews on tape.

In fact he was reluctant to do anything of the sort. It

was the old story of the difference between a naturalist and a behaviourist; the one learns about his subjects in the wild, the other prefers the totally alien environment of a laboratory where, in a carefully designed box, the creature, whatever it is, is put through a programme of party tricks.

For Wycliffe, Ventonbos was the wild.

The law prescribes how formal interrogations shall take place, and he would come to that. But not yet.

They set out in Wycliffe's car with Lucy driving. Neither of the women had been to Ventonbos and, for once, Wycliffe had to give directions. He brought them successfully and with a certain pride to the track which led off the road to the house.

The sun shone; it was warm, windless and silent.

Lucy parked under the arching trees in the yard and they got out.

Iris said, 'There's nobody home.'

They went round to the front and found Dr Cross seated on a bench by the front door, reading. 'Ah! Mr Wycliffe.' Without enthusiasm.

Wycliffe thought that the distress at the news he had brought on his first visit seemed to have evaporated, or been overlaid. He sensed that he was now facing a considered strategy.

He said, 'Let me introduce my colleagues: Detective Sergeant Lane; Detective Constable Thorn.'

Dr Florence looked the two policewomen over with an approving eye. 'You'd better come inside, I suppose. All three of you.'

Chapter Eleven

They were shepherded into the big room.

Dr Florence said, 'I'll get Isobel.'

She was gone some minutes. Although the sun shone outside, the light in the room was ecclesiastical, matching the silence.

Iris Thorn said, 'Can anybody actually *live* in this?'

Lucy Lane's contribution, looking up at the doctor's portrait, was, 'I don't think I'd want to live with anything quite so explicit about me.'

The two women arrived from their mutual briefing. Formal introductions over, Wycliffe was smoothly incisive. 'I want to talk to Dr Cross if I may. Perhaps you, Miss Wilde, will show DS Lane and DC Thorn the upstairs rooms? We shall cause as little disturbance as possible.'

Through an exchange of glances Dr Florence and Isobel ensured consensus, then Isobel left with Lucy Lane and Iris Thorn. Wycliffe would have given a lot to have been a fly on the wall as that encounter developed.

Dr Florence sat down, hands resting on the knees of her tartan trousers. Falsely brisk, she said, 'Well, Mr Wycliffe?'

'I want to ask you about a possible connection between you and Morwenna's family, the Barkers.'

Caught off-base, Dr Florence recovered quickly. 'What sort of connection? Perhaps you will explain.'

'At one time, in your professional capacity, you attended a number of births in what was then St Agatha's Nursing Home, at Tresillian. Is that so?'

'It is a matter of record.' Snappish.

'Do you recall a young unmarried girl, Bessie Barker? The date would have been towards the end of July or the beginning of August in nineteen sixty-four.'

Pursed lips then: 'You are playing with me, Superintendent. It was the thirtieth of July. You obviously know that my husband and I adopted that girl's child. It was done in a perfectly legal and proper manner and, as you must have learned or guessed, that child was Julian.'

Not a lady to fight a lost battle. Wycliffe tried again. 'The baby was deformed at birth?'

A spasm of resentment, instantly suppressed. 'Yes. And you are wondering why we chose to adopt that particular child. I will tell you quite plainly. One: we could not have a child of our own. Two: we knew the child needed special care which we were in a position to provide. And three: my husband, as his published work will show, had a professional interest in the psychology of deformity.'

A formidable woman. Appear open. Nothing to hide. Give more than is asked for, when it doesn't matter. But such people can trip over their own cleverness.

And was there an element of contempt in her

reference to the husband who wanted a deformed child as an object of study?

From where he sat Wycliffe could look down the steep slope through a narrow gap in the trees to the waters of the creek. As he watched, Julian, carrying a sweep-net, emerged from the trees into the gap and started towards the house.

'When was your son told who his natural parents were?'

An irritable gesture. 'I don't understand, Mr Wycliffe, how all this is linked to what happened to the poor girl.'

Wycliffe was patient. 'Morwenna was obsessively concerned with what she believed to be the injustice suffered by her father. But Julian was her brother, and might reasonably have shared her concern. It is clearly important to know to what extent he identified with her.'

Even to him the reasoning sounded specious but it was effective. Dr Florence responded, 'He was told quite early on that he was adopted, but he was given the impression that we did not know the identity of his natural parents.' She added quickly, 'You will understand that I left all that to Raymond – my husband. He was the one best qualified to make such judgements.'

A washing of hands.

'And when did Julian discover that he was related to the Barkers?'

'It was years later; not long before Raymond left us.' She crossed her legs in a vigorous movement. 'In fact he may already have decided to go at that time. His behaviour had become very strange and this could have been his way of closing the account. At any rate, it was then that he told Julian the identity of his natural parents.'

'That must have been shortly after Barker, his natural father, was sent to prison for manslaughter.'

'Yes.'

Wycliffe dotted i-s and crossed t-s: 'So Julian, at the age of twenty-five, learned that for many years his natural parents and his young sister had been living within a couple or three miles of his home. And at the same time that his father was starting a prison sentence for manslaughter.'

'Yes.'

'The news must have come as a shock. Did he resent its nature and timing?'

Dr Florence spread her hands. 'It's impossible to tell with Julian. At first I thought it had meant little to him, but as time went by it became obvious that he was becoming increasingly interested in the Barkers.'

There were footsteps in the hall; the door of the room was open and Julian was framed in the doorway, holding his net, with a canvas bag slung over his shoulder.

Nobody spoke. It was like an episode in a charade. Julian stood there looking at them, and Wycliffe had the impression not of a vacant stare but of intelligent scrutiny. After a moment or two the young man turned away and continued down the passage.

In an impulsive movement which seemed to be her reflex reaction to stress, Dr Florence swept back her hair with both hands. And when she spoke it was as though there had been no interruption. 'I can tell you that it was a very great surprise when he turned up one day and said that he had made contact with his sister, and that he had invited her here.'

'The girl knew nothing of their relationship?'

'Apparently not.'

'Had he told her?'

'I'm not sure that he ever told her. I don't know.'

'You were surprised when he brought Morwenna here. Were you upset?'

'Not upset – no. Isobel and I were concerned – worried at first, I suppose. But we need not have been. Morwenna seemed to be good for him although her own situation was very sad. More than sad, it was tragic. The misfortunes of her family and her debilitating illness were combining to spoil her life.'

'But she became a regular visitor.'

'Yes, and a welcome one. We thought that at last Julian had found a companion.'

Wycliffe was trying to sort out his ideas. He had been treated to the Dr Florence version, carefully prepared and edited, though not necessarily false for that. The woman was intelligent, and she realized that a possible criminal charge against somebody might lurk somewhere behind the smooth talk.

He doubted whether he had heard half the truth about Morwenna's leaving or, for that matter, anything like the whole story of the disappearing husband, but those doubts were a long way from any accusation of criminal involvement.

When they reached the top of the stairs Lucy said, 'We shall start in the room used by Morwenna.'

Isobel took them to the little room at the front of the house which Wycliffe had already seen. She said, 'This is how Morwenna left it last Sunday. Nothing has been disturbed. She always kept some clothes and a few other things here, and last Sunday was no different.'

The two policewomen set to work. Everything from the wardrobe and from the drawers was removed and laid upon the bed. For a time Isobel stood in the doorway watching, fiddling with her pearls, but she soon tired and they were left alone.

What was laid out on the bed didn't amount to a lot, a couple of summer dresses, two or three jumpers, a couple of skirts, a pair of trousers, a blouse, underclothes, stockings, slippers and shoes.

Add to that basic toilet gear, an empty handbag and half a dozen paperbacks.

Iris summed up: 'She went for quality, I'll say that for her. No end-of-season sale stuff in this lot. Anyway, like the woman said, she seems to have counted on coming back.'

Lucy said, 'We'll give the other rooms a once-over.'

At random they picked one across the passage at the back of the house. As soon as they opened the door Iris said, 'Isobel.'

It was the room of an indulged or self-indulgent young woman; a dedicated virgin. Furniture and fabrics were expensive and restrained, oak and oatmeal everywhere. There were subdued prints in matching frames on the walls, and a shelf or two of books, perfectly aligned. There was a writing table and two or three chairs.

Iris said, 'A change from our Wenna's room. This lot must have set the bank balance back a bit. You can't help wondering what Dr Flo keeps inside her tartan trews but she's obviously willing to pay for her pleasures.'

Lucy was going through the books: literature from the female pen, Jane to Virginia with an experimental sprinkling of the modern explicits.

Iris said, 'I was thinking of our Morwenna. Poor little mug. Do you think she could have been competition for Isobel?'

They moved on. Another large room at the back; this time Julian's, without a doubt. At a guess, furnished with bits and pieces gathered at different times from all over the house.

The bookshelves overflowed on to the top of the chest of drawers. Lucy went through the shelves: entomological texts with bundles of journals and transactions of the Society. Among the non-scientific literature Lucy found the works of Lewis Carroll with supporting biographies and critical studies. They said something about the young man. Did he see himself as one of the characters? Was he the wide-eyed Alice? The anarchic Mad Hatter? The cynical Cheshire Cat? Or the lugubrious Mock Turtle? Perhaps Humpty Dumpty on his wall.

Iris was looking at a framed photograph on the mantelpiece, an ordinary family snapshot, enlarged.

'That's Morwenna with her family – when she was young.'

Neither of them had met Julian, neither of them had heard his approach, but there he was. 'I'm Julian and this is my room.' A statement; no hint of aggression.

He joined Iris and took the photograph in his hand. He pointed. 'That's her father – and mine, George Barker . . . He cut his throat when they let him out of prison . . .' There was a long pause before he added, 'And it was Morwenna who found him . . .' He shuddered. 'Horrible!'

He pointed to the woman. 'That's Bessie – our mother. She died. Morwenna was sure that she died of grief for her husband . . . And that's Nicky, our cousin. He was an orphan.'

Another long pause before he said, 'And that's Morwenna, my sister. She was fourteen when that was taken and twenty-three when I met her for the first time. And that was by chance.'

'You were obviously very fond of her.'

There were tears in his eyes. A moment or two went by while he seemed to study the photograph, then, 'They're all dead now. All except Nicky.'

Iris changed the subject. 'I suppose your mother told you why we are here?'

'No, but I know that you are from the police and that you are trying to find out how and why Morwenna died.'

Lucy intervened. 'We are trying to find out what we can about her life while she was here.'

'Isn't that the same thing?'

Lucy asked, rather too sharply, 'In what way?'

'I suppose her life here must have played some part in her death.'

There was an awkward pause, then Iris changed the subject. 'You study insects.' Half a question; half a statement.

The mild china-blue eyes seemed to be assessing the motive behind the question. Was he being patronized? He must have decided that he was not, for he answered, 'Flies mainly. Silly, isn't it?'

'Silly? I don't think so. Are people who study birds or fish, whales or chimpanzees, silly?'

He smiled and his pale face was transformed. 'Would you like to see where I work?'

Iris turned to Lucy Lane. 'Sarge?'

'Why not?'

Iris was taken downstairs to the small room behind the kitchen with its bench and its bottles, its microscope and its shallow drawers.

Iris was shown the contents of the drawers with their regimented displays of flies arranged according to species, genera and families.

'Are they all flies?'

'They are all Diptera – Di-ptera – that is to say, two-winged flies, and all collected in the garden and surrounding woods and fields.'

Iris admired.

'And this is one that I took early this morning.' He picked up a small specimen tube in which a winged insect crawled sluggishly over the glass wall. Its body was patterned with black and yellow markings.

'It looks a bit like a wasp to me.'

'That's the idea. It's a fly that looks vaguely like a wasp, enough to make a hungry bird think twice. Biologists call it "warning colouration" and "mimicry".'

'You mean it's deliberate?'

'It depends what you mean by deliberate but we won't go into that for your first lesson.' A quick smile. 'Anyway, this one is a hover-fly called *Catabomba pyrastri*.'

'Poor thing. It sounds like exploding spaghetti.'

A chuckle which, Iris guessed, was a rare phenomenon.

He seemed to be capable of rapid changes of mood. Here was a different Julian from the one who had mused over the Barker family photograph a few minutes earlier.

Iris said, 'Did you study biology?'

'I've never really studied anything much.'

'But you must have gone to school.'

'Sporadically. They tried me at a boarding school but I was asked to leave. And in the day schools it didn't work out too well.'

He broke off, looking at her, questioning. 'You're black and I'm crippled. To some extent we're both in the same boat – targets for political correctness – or the other thing. I hardly know which is worse.'

He picked up the specimen tube containing the live fly. 'I must deal with this.' He reached down a wide-mouthed bottle containing what appeared to be cotton wool overlaid with plastic gauze. He removed the stopper and a smell of ether pervaded the little room. He dropped the already torpid fly into the bottle and replaced the stopper. 'Ethyl acetate. I find that's the best killing agent.'

The little fly crawled slowly and aimlessly over the gauze.

'Don't you *feel* anything when you do that?'

A quick look. 'I used to, but one becomes inured.' He turned to look at her. 'Don't you find that people are like that? Repetition soon chases away scruples, and one has to be careful about going down that road.'

He stood looking down at his fly which had finally

come to rest on the gauze. 'I've known what it's like to be on the receiving end. I wasn't killed in a bottle and pinned out in a tray, but I sometimes wonder if that mightn't have been preferable.'

'Your father?'

'The man who adopted me.'

Iris tried again. 'Do you get on well with Isobel?'

'Oh, yes.' He hesitated. 'We were like brother and sister until I found my real sister.'

He looked at Iris. 'I think it's time we closed the confessional, don't you?' And he was not smiling.

In the big front room Wycliffe was saying, 'Now we come to the Sunday – last Sunday – when Morwenna left.'

Dr Florence frowned. 'I told you. She came and went as she wished. More often than not she went off walking, but sometimes she took her car.'

'And she did so on Sunday?'

'Yes.'

'When she didn't return during the day, weren't you concerned?'

'No. Once or twice in the days before she left, she mentioned the possibility that she might make contact with her aunt in St Ives and I assumed she had done that.'

In the context of this house and these people, it was believable – just.

He could hear Lucy Lane and Iris Thorn in the hall and he decided that, for the moment, he had got as far as he was likely to. At some stage there would have to be a showdown, pressure would need to be applied, but not before they had more leverage. Premature formal questioning which achieves nothing can be a stumbling block to the future.

'Stir thoroughly, bring to the boil, and allow to simmer.' It made tactical sense, and with luck he could go home for at least part of the weekend. What was more, with operations suspended the over-time bill would come down, giving pleasure in high places.

He joined Lucy and Iris in the car and was driven back to the incident room.

Arrangements were completed for a weekend stand-off and in the early evening there was a winding-up session. Present: Det. Supt Wycliffe, DI Kersey, DS Lane and DC Thorn.

Wycliffe looked weary; Kersey sat back in his chair apparently asleep; Lucy Lane turned the pages of her notebook, and Iris Thorn sat, trim, prim and composed.

Wycliffe said, 'First let's hear what Lucy and Iris have to say.'

The two women reported in a lively blend of facts, opinions, impressions and asides. Exactly the sort of thing he could appreciate.

Lucy said, 'Of course Dr Florence and Isobel Wilde are in a lesbian relationship and if that started before the husband left I suppose it could have had something to do with him going.'

'Any hint of tensions between the three women? Could Isobel have seen Morwenna as dangerous competition?'

Lucy considered. 'After Julian took Iris to see his flies, Isobel turned up again, and I talked to her alone.

As to Morwenna being competition, it's possible, but I had no impression of any serious rift between the doctor and Isobel.

'At a guess, I'd say that Isobel has a very soft spot for Julian. She certainly had no room for Dr Raymond. She was careful in what she said, but there was no love lost there.'

Iris put in, 'Nor between Julian and his stand-in papa. Nothing but bitterness. And no secret made of it. It seems that he was treated as a specimen, like a laboratory rat, sometimes useful but of no real consequence.'

Lucy frowned. 'It sounds absurd, but I had an idea that Isobel was most concerned about something quite different from the things we talked about. I felt that I was missing the point, but I still haven't a clue as to what that point might have been.'

Wycliffe turned to Iris. 'What about Julian's attitude to Morwenna?'

Iris was emphatic. 'Oh, Julian loved his sister and it was one of the things he held against Raymond, that he'd never been allowed to know his true family.'

Wycliffe sat back in his chair. 'From the start of this affair we've been dogged by uncertainty as to what we are about. A Missing Persons routine concerning Morwenna Barker involved us with her father's conviction on a manslaughter charge six years earlier, and with her attempts to dole out what she considered to be justice to the bookseller.'

Wycliffe sipped the current brand of incident room coffee, made a face and put the mug aside. 'The discovery of Morwenna's body in the quarry pool seemed to provide a focus, but there was uncertainty as to exactly how she died, and not only how, but why. If she was murdered, what was the motive?

'The usual mix of inquiries and luck led us to the set-up at Ventonbos, where the girl spent a good deal of her time in the weeks and months preceding her death. And here again we come across the Barker theme in the person of his natural son.'

Wycliffe paused, 'And if you choose to look at it that way, there's an odd parallel. Julian, who lost his natural father without knowing him, also lost his father by adoption.'

Kersey stirred himself. 'I'm not clear about what, exactly, you're saying, sir.'

Wycliffe snapped. 'Then you're still one step ahead of me, Doug. I'm not even clear about what I'm trying to say.'

Sometimes when Wycliffe was less than sure of his ground he could be irritated by Kersey.

Then he grinned, good humour restored. 'Obviously I haven't struck a chord. Anyway, I've had enough and I'm going home.'

Chapter Twelve

It was dark when Wycliffe arrived home. The night was still, and the navigation lights in the estuary were reflected in smooth water. In the clean air the glare from the city to the north failed for once to dim the stars. Helen heard his car and came to the door. The ritual kiss.

In the kitchen: 'You look worried.'

'I suppose I am. Anyway I feel that I'm getting nowhere fast. On the face of it we're investigating the death of a girl who ended up in her car at the bottom of a quarry pool. A tragedy, but the sort of thing we can come to grips with.'

'But?'

'In fact we seem to have uncovered a can of worms.'

A cup of tea, a large cup. Tea made by pouring boiling water on loose tea-leaves in a warmed earthenware pot. Wait three minutes for the mixture to brew, then pour into your cup where there's already a little milk. No sugar. Sit back, enjoy and wait for your troubles to melt away.

It almost worked. He hung around in the kitchen, theoretically helping Helen to prepare a scratch meal; in fact adding sherry to the tea.

They had their meal while listening to a CD of Helen's choosing – Verdi. And went to bed.

A restless night. Usually his dreams were vague fantasy projections of reality in which the figures of the daily round were rarely identifiable. Tonight was different. He dreamed of Dr Florence Cross, her features sharpened to the point of caricature. Seated in her usual place, below her portrait, she was looking at him with a derisory smile.

No words were exchanged, but after an interval Isobel came into the room. Her plump schoolgirlish figure was naked except for her pearls, and she stood, looking from one to the other. In the end she said, 'Haven't you told him?'

'No.'

Isobel seemed irritated, 'Why not? We can't go on like this!'

Saturday 19 August

He must have slept longer than he thought for when he woke it was broad daylight and the little bedside clock said five minutes to seven. With extreme, but fruitless caution he eased himself out of bed.

Half awake, Helen said, 'What's the matter? Where are you going? It's Saturday, isn't it?'

'I'm not going anywhere. I can't get to sleep again so I thought I'd get up and make some tea. Do you want a cup?'

'I'd rather go back to sleep.'

Downstairs he switched on the kettle then walked in the garden. In the early-morning light, looking down towards the estuary through the fringing trees, he thought that the scene was not so very different from the view out of the window of that large, littered room at Ventonbos.

But this was *alive*, while at Ventonbos, despite the burgeoning growth, the atmosphere was funereal, reminiscent of a neglected cemetery.

'Haven't you told him? . . . Why not? We can't go on like this!' – Isobel's words in his dream, as she stood there, wearing her pearls, her strangely immature body revealed in its nakedness.

Wycliffe shirked speculation on a Freudian interpretation and tried to relate the dream to his daytime world. He failed. His dreams, however pertinent they seemed, rarely yielded to logic.

Macavity the Second came out of the shrubbery and started rubbing round his legs, purring. Cupboard love, of course. So he went back indoors, fed the beast and made himself that promised cup of tea.

Drinking his tea, he was interrupted by the telephone. The duty CID officer at headquarters: 'Sorry to trouble you, sir, but I've got a guy on the line demanding to speak to you. He's probably a nutcase, but somehow—'

'What's his name?'

'Julian Cross, he says.'

'Let me talk to him, and tape it.' Common practice for such transferred calls.

'You're through, sir.'

'It's Julian.'

'You want to talk to me?'

'Yes. You must come down . . . It's about Morwenna.'

223

'Are you speaking from home?'

'Yes . . . You must come down. It was my fault that Morwenna died . . . I told her . . . If only I'd kept quiet she would be here now. But I didn't want more secrets. Not between us. There have been too many in this house.'

There was a long pause, followed by a despairing, 'I don't know what to do . . . I just don't know!'

The line went dead but it was some time before Wycliffe dropped the telephone. Even then he hesitated, but finally he looked up and dialled the Ventonbos number.

The teeth-grinding ringing tone was answered at last. Isobel, irritated, snapped, 'Yes?'

'Superintendent Wycliffe. I would like to speak to Julian if he's available, please.'

'Oh. I'll see.' A long wait. He thought he heard Dr Florence's voice. Had she been got out of bed? Then, 'I can't find him; he must have gone off somewhere. He often does in the early morning.'

'It doesn't matter. Thank you.'

As he replaced the phone Helen, who had come downstairs and was listening, said, 'What was that about?'

'I don't know. Something's happening there and I think I shall have to go down. I'm sorry.'

'I suppose I should be used to it, and since you came home last night you've only been half here anyway.'

Breakfast, the atmosphere still a little charged, but improving.

Helen saw him to his car, 'You'll be back this evening?'

224

'Promise.'

Wycliffe, who had never been averse to making the same mistake twice, decided not to involve any of the team at this stage. He arrived at Ventonbos ninety minutes later, pleased with himself, and parked in the yard. Julian's Escort was there.

Half-past ten. The back door was ajar. He knocked, then walked in.

Isobel met him in the passage, in obvious distress. 'Julian was out when you called and he hasn't come back. But look in there!'

They were standing by the open door of Julian's laboratory. Everything was as Wycliffe remembered it except that the glass lid of a specimen drawer on the workbench had been smashed in. Jagged pieces of the thin glass lodged between and on the regimented specimens below, and some of them had been crushed. There was blood on the glass, on the white cork-lining of the drawer, and on the bench top. More blood had dripped to the floor.

'You don't know what happened?'

'No. We found it not long before you came. It's what worried us. Julian is hardly ever around when we come down in the morning. So there was nothing unusual in that, but Florence noticed blood on the floor in the passage and in the hall, and she traced it back to here. After we'd made sure he wasn't in the house she went looking for him outside. He must have cut himself quite badly.'

Wycliffe went through to the hall and out by the front door. He had no idea where to look or what to do, but then he saw Dr Florence emerge from the wilderness into the gap which ran down to the shore.

She came toiling up the slope and he went to meet her. She was unnaturally flushed. Leaves and twigs clung to her woollen jumper and her trousers.

'I've found him.' She stopped, striving to recover her breath. 'He's down there . . . And he's dead.' She seemed to accept Wycliffe's presence without question. 'You'd better let me show you.'

Wycliffe followed her. Halfway to the creek she turned off to the right along a narrow path snagged by trailing brambles. There had been overnight rain and they were spattered with droplets as they pushed their way through. The path ended in a clearing, overhung by trees.

Julian was slumped on the ground, his head propped against a low wall of moss-covered bricks, as though he had slipped from a sitting position. The posture of the body, exaggerated by its deformity, seemed grotesque. His head was thrust forward on to his chest, and his fine, almost colourless, hair was caught in the sunlight. His shirt was soaked in blood, some of which had not had time to clot.

And, as if in a final irony, there were flies.

Wycliffe crouched beside him and Dr Florence snapped, 'He's dead, man! Do you think I didn't check? He's cut his throat. You can't see the actual wounds without lifting his head, but there are two gashes: one to the left of the larynx opened the jugular, the other, below it, severed the trachea.'

A woman standing over the body of her adopted son. But a moment later the stridency had gone from her voice and she spoke quietly. 'I had to make sure. I mean, although it was obvious that he was past help . . .'

Wycliffe had known too many instances of apparent callousness from people in shock to be critical.

But Florence Cross was not, in any case, a woman to be judged by ordinary standards.

An open (grimly appropriate) cut-throat razor lay by the limp right hand and the hand itself had bled from a number of small cuts across the knuckles and lower joints of the fingers.

Reflective, Dr Florence said, 'He used that razor for cutting wax-embedded sections for the microscope. He was good at it . . .' A moment later she added, 'He must have smashed the glass lid of that drawer with his fist.'

And later still, with more sentiment than she had so far shown. 'This was his favourite spot. He used to come here as a child.'

So much for that phone call. Made in desperation. If he, Wycliffe, had responded differently, could this have been prevented? And what had Julian really wanted to say?

Now routine took precedence over all else; the prescribed routine for a sudden and violent death: the police surgeon, the mortuary people, the coroner. DI Lister would handle the drill but he had to be told.

For Wycliffe it was a question of how this presumed suicide was related to Morwenna's death. The two women would have to be questioned and statements taken. The weekend break which had barely started was over.

Sanders, the police surgeon, long, lean, ex-RAF, got up from kneeling beside the body, brushing his trousers. Wycliffe had met him before; they were about the same age.

'There's nothing much I can say that isn't obvious. They can take him away.'

'I want Franks to have a look at him on the table.'

Raised eyebrows. 'Surely you've no doubt that he killed himself?'

'No, and I don't want anybody else to have any either.'

Last evening he was complaining that the inquiry lacked a defined focus. Well, he could say that again.

He needed the team. If not to investigate a suicide, at least to discover how that suicide fitted into the pattern. Kersey would draw the shortest straw. He had stayed on at the hotel in Falmouth and brought Joan, his wife, down to join him for the weekend. Lucy Lane, who seemed to have relatives conveniently scattered throughout the south-west, was staying with a cousin near Penzance.

By early afternoon Wycliffe had his team: Kersey, Lucy Lane and Iris Thorn. They had taken over the Ventonbos dining room as a temporary base. It had not been in use for years but the furniture remained, and there was even a little pile of dinner plates on the sideboard. There was also dust.

They sat on balloon-backed chairs at a draw-table.

A strange briefing.

Wycliffe gave an account of his morning. 'I shall be talking to the two women but I'm leaving the rest to you, Doug. Lister is looking after the suicide routine but keep in touch. Obviously there must be a thorough search of the young man's room and his lab.'

Wycliffe wound up, reminding himself as much as the others. 'It was on Thursday morning that we discovered the Ventonbos angle; it's now only Saturday. We've opened up a new line, and inevitably there's a lot of follow-up to be done. If we need to bring in more bodies then we must; but let's see how we go.'

A few minutes later Wycliffe was in the big room with the two women.

The atmosphere was unreal. Isobel had been weeping, and from time to time she dabbed her eyes with a handkerchief rolled up into a ball. There was tension. Dr Florence sat, her body rigid, alert to every move.

Wycliffe made soothing noises, then, 'I want you to tell me precisely what happened this morning before I arrived.'

Isobel looked at Dr Florence before speaking. 'We don't get up very early. Julian is always up well before us.' She spoke haltingly, pausing to dab her eyes. 'The first I heard was the telephone ringing and I went down to answer it . . . Of course it was you, wanting to speak to Julian. Then Florence came down and we looked for him but, as you know, we didn't find him.'

Dr Florence intervened. 'But there was nothing unusual in that. He often went off in the early morning and we generally didn't see him until midday.'

Isobel, tentative, ventured a question. 'Why did you want him?'

'It was he who wanted me. He had telephoned me through my headquarters, apparently as a matter of urgency. He said that he wanted to talk to me personally, but that I must come down. He implied that he had something to tell me, but when I tried to question him he rang off.'

Quite a sizeable stone in the pool. Dr Florence leaned forward in her seat. Isobel looked startled and incredulous.

Wycliffe asked, 'Have you any idea what he wanted to tell me?'

Isobel shook her head, and Dr Florence said, 'I can't imagine! He's been very strange since Morwenna left.'

'Perhaps you will carry on with your account of what happened.'

Dr Florence said, 'There isn't much to tell. It must have been around ten when I noticed blood on the stone floor of the passage and hall. I traced it back to Julian's workroom and, of course, I found the specimen drawer with its smashed lid.' She spread her hands. 'It was obvious that Julian had suffered one of his fits.'

'Fits?'

Dr Florence was flustered. 'That's what I said, but I wasn't using the word in any medical sense. Julian was subject to spells of extreme depression and frustration, which he sometimes relieved by some such pointless act. Once he kicked in a panel of the back door. When anything like that happened it was a great shock, coming from someone normally so quiet and amenable.'

For Wycliffe it was a strange, almost unnerving experience. He had to remind himself that the young man they were discussing with such objectivity had, only a few hours before, taken his life in a particularly violent and bloody fashion. And this had occurred within a couple of hundred yards of where they were sitting.

Wycliffe was instinctively repelled, but it made an unpleasant task easier. Even without Julian's cryptic phone call it would have been inconceivable that his suicide was unrelated to his sister's death and he had no qualms about exploiting the connection in order to draw out the two women.

Paradoxically his manner became more relaxed and conversational. 'There will be an inquest, with questions concerning Julian's state of mind as well as the actual circumstances leading to his death. His telephone call to me will, of course, be relevant.'

A pause to allow this to sink in. Then, 'The adjourned inquest into Morwenna's death will soon be resumed, and the two will overlap in matters of substance. Of course, the object of my inquiry is to discover how, why and by whom Morwenna Barker was murdered.'

Outside sunshine alternated with cloud, and in the changing half-lights and shadows of the cluttered room the faces of the two women stood out, pale and almost luminous.

Wycliffe was in no hurry and they waited on his words, perhaps wary of anticipating questions that might not be asked.

'According to the account you gave me, Morwenna left here for the last time alone, and of her own accord, on Sunday morning.'

There was no response, and Wycliffe allowed some time to elapse before adding, 'I have difficulty in accepting that version. We know that Morwenna left here on Sunday morning. We know where she went, what she did and what she said. But I am satisfied that she returned and I am also satisfied that Julian called me because he felt driven to tell me the truth; truth which might have involved a confession or an accusation.'

The two women looked at each other. Then Dr Florence almost spluttered, 'You have no right . . . !'

Isobel said nothing but her fingers were working overtime on the little rolled-up handkerchief.

Wycliffe continued, 'What I'm saying is that you will be key witnesses at both inquiries, and your account of Morwenna's leaving will be regarded as critical. You are likely to be subjected to very close questioning and I suggest that in your own interests you should consider carefully what you will say.

'Julian's telephone call to me will be treated as significant.'

There was silence. Isobel shifted uneasily in her chair; Dr Florence rested her long bony hands on bony knees and stared straight in front.

Wycliffe continued, 'I mention this now because, so far, I have not asked you to attend for an interview on the record. That has to be done, and quite soon. Before that happens I want you to understand the searching nature of the questions you will be asked.'

A long pause before Dr Florence said, 'We must do what we have to.'

Wycliffe left. In the hall he took a deep breath. He was playing with fire, but for the first time he felt that he was getting to grips.

He found Kersey in the dining room. 'Lucy and Iris are having their second go at Julian's room. I've fixed things with Lister, and he's dealing with the suicide.'

Wycliffe said, 'Let's take a walk to the creek.'

They walked down the steep slope between the trees.

Wycliffe said, 'Your first visit to Ventonbos; what's your impression?'

Kersey grinned. 'A good site for a crematorium if they need one. It's got the atmosphere. Did you get anywhere with the women?'

Wycliffe told him.

Kersey's rubbery features creased in thought. Finally he said, 'Well, you've baited the hook, sir. We shall have to see what we catch.'

They arrived at the path leading off to the clearing and followed it. The undergrowth had been cut back and access was easy. 'This is where he was found, sprawled on the ground, his head propped against that little wall.'

Kersey looked at the vague impression left by the body. 'Poor devil! I've often wondered what it takes for a man to end things that way. I can't imagine it.'

'It's the way his father chose.'

'His father? . . . Oh, yes! It's difficult to think of him as Barker's son . . . And that makes it all the odder.'

Wycliffe was examining the structure of which the little wall of mossy bricks formed a part. The brambles which covered it were in full leaf and carried clusters of luscious-looking blackberries. The bricks seemed to form a circle, four or five feet in diameter, built into the slope. Poking with a stick through several inches of soil he encountered a hard surface. It felt like timber.

He turned to Kersey. 'It's a well!'

Kersey joined him. 'So what?'

'Ventonbos. Venton: Cornish for a well; bos:

Cornish for, among other things, a dwelling place. A dwelling place with a well.'

'Big deal, but I still don't get it.'

'Do you think Tom Reed knew about this?'

Understanding dawned. 'You think . . . It's worth a try. It shouldn't be difficult to uncover—'

'Let's see what Tom has to say first.'

They walked back up the slope and around the house to the police car parked in the yard. A moment or two later Wycliffe was speaking to Tom Reed.

'The well? Yes, I know about the well. We thought of that and had it dipped, or whatever it is you do with wells. Nothing, beyond a few sherds from broken pitchers, the odd bucket and a lot of mud.'

'Was it overgrown?'

'No. It seems the doctor – Raymond, that is, fancied the water, but it had recently been analysed and condemned because there were bugs in it.'

Kersey said, 'So that's that. Pity!'

Lucy Lane and Iris had found nothing of significance. Their haul consisted of an album of snapshots of the Barker family, which Morwenna must have given Julian. Interesting, but not evidence.

Wycliffe was on the point of getting into his car when he stopped and looked at his watch. 'It's still only a little after five.' He turned to Lucy Lane. 'You and Iris get back. I'll be in touch later.'

When the two had left, Kersey said, 'What's this about?'

'The well. We've got close on four hours before the light goes and I can't bring myself to walk away from here without at least making an effort to find out if there's anything down there.'

234

'But Tom Reed checked the well.'

'I know, but we'll see for ourselves. We need a bill-hook or something, and a shovel. I noticed some tools just inside the door of the shed.'

'Shouldn't we tell the inmates?'

'No. It would only worry them.'

Kersey laughed. 'I sometimes think I've never really got to know you.'

'So you're on?'

'Do I have a choice?'

They found a slashing hook, a shovel and a mattock. Wycliffe fetched a torch from his car. If they were seen, there was no attempt to question what they were doing. They made their way round the house and down to the clearing.

The sun shone, there was a gentle breeze out of the south, but soon it would be evening. Out in the creek a motor launch chugged expensively, nosing around in the shallows before returning, wisely, to the channel.

The job was easier than they expected, the brambles had a poor hold in the shallow soil covering the well-head, and in under half an hour the wooden cover was exposed. All at the cost of a few scratches and several curses.

The well-head had been capped with stout planks, shaped and battened together allowing a square hinged cover in the middle. The hinges were rusted so that when they lifted the cover they came away with it, but there was the well . . .

The summer had been dry and levels everywhere were low; but the water, gleaming darkly, was no more than ten or twelve feet down.

Kersey said, 'I can't see anything.'

Wycliffe shone his torch and the beam picked up what looked like a large parcel, wrapped in black plastic, which appeared to float just below the surface.

Kersey said, 'Looks to me like somebody's rubbish in a bin-bag.'

'Maybe, but I'm going to have it out, whatever it is.'

'This evening?'

'No, we shall need somebody with a ladder and some sort of gear. It's a job for the wet-suit brigade. We'll come back tomorrow, properly organized.'

Justifiably or not, Wycliffe felt relieved, almost light-hearted. 'We're getting there, Doug.'

Chapter Thirteen

At half-past nine in the morning Wycliffe, with
Lucy Lane driving, arrived at Ventonbos and parked
in the yard. Kersey, accompanied by DC Curnow
and a photographer, followed in an unmarked police
car.

Two PCs trained for underwater recovery were due
to arrive shortly, with their van.

Wycliffe said, 'I know you see this as a bit excessive,
Doug; all this deployment to recover a bin-bag of
rubbish.'

Kersey grinned. 'We shall see, sir.'

The old house had the knack of looking even
gloomier in sunshine. They went to the back door
which was open, and Dr Florence came down the
passage looking worried, but sounding aggressive. 'I
didn't expect you here today. I thought that on a
Sunday we might be allowed a little peace.'

Wycliffe was formal. 'I have to tell you that I've
arranged for the well to be investigated.'

It sounded absurd; but was there a better way of
putting it?

'The well?' Very sharp. Surprise or alarm? It was
hard to tell.

'The well in the clearing where Julian's body was found.'

'I know what you're talking about, but I can see no possible connection between it and Julian's tragic death. The well was sealed off years ago.'

Wycliffe said nothing, and she demanded, 'Do you have any right to do this sort of thing?'

'You are entitled to refuse, but if you do I shall obtain a warrant.'

She turned away without asking the obvious question.

Wycliffe fetched a torch from his car. 'I'm going on down, Doug. I'll leave you to deal with the wet-suits.'

He reached the clearing. The scene was idyllic. A day for sailing on the Helford, not for exploring some disused well up one of its creeks. To add to the incongruity, church bells were ringing.

Everything was as he and Kersey had left it. Standing on the timber capping, Wycliffe lifted the hinged cover and stared down at the dark water. He shone his torch, and there was the black plastic bundle, gleaming faintly in the torch beam.

He stepped off the capping and looked down at the stubbly grass where Julian's crippled body had lain. There, in the dappled sunlight, his back propped against the moss-covered bricks, he had ended his life. He had come prepared. But for how long had he sat there, agonizing, before he could translate despair into courage for the last act?

'It was my fault that Morwenna died . . . If only I'd kept quiet . . .'

But what did he tell?

A commotion up the slope, and Kersey arrived

followed by two men in shirts and jeans. Both were lean and swarthy; they could have been taken for twins.

'PCs Sparks and Wills, sir. We've come for a preliminary look. See what gear we need to bring down. Our truck is up in the yard.'

They inspected the well-head, peered down the hatch and examined the timber capping. 'Have to get some of that off but there's not much to it. Plenty of room to work off the ladder. Piece of cake!'

'We'll fetch our gear, sir.'

In a very short time they were back with their equipment which included an aluminium ladder, a coil of nylon rope, and a device which, anchored to the ground, could extend an arm with a pulley over the well. There was also a sling which looked like a leg-pad for a cricketing Goliath.

'We shall wrap that round whatever it is to avoid damage, sir.'

When part of the timber capping had been removed, they let down the ladder into the well, hooking it to the brick parapet. PC Sparks had drawn the short straw. In his suit, with a safety harness, but with no helmet or goggles, he climbed over the parapet and disappeared.

A few moments later his voice resonated up the well. 'The sling, Nick!'

The sling was lowered on the nylon rope, fed over the pulley. For several minutes sounds came from the well: splashing water, grunts and imprecations. Then, 'I'm coming up!'

PC Sparks emerged, 'back to grass', as the miners used to say. He stepped over the parapet and stood shaking himself like a dog. 'Well, it's a body and it's wrapped in plastic which has been tied round the neck, waist, thighs and ankles. I've secured the sling at an angle so that it won't foul the sides. Now all we've got to do is haul it out.'

Wycliffe asked, 'Is it still submerged?'

'Half and half.'

'Then leave it there until the mortuary people arrive. Lying about in the sun isn't going to improve it, or Dr Franks' temper.'

Wycliffe turned to Kersey. 'Get on your mobile to the mortuary people, Doug, and tell them it's urgent. We also want a photographer. I'll talk to Franks, if they can find him. I dropped word that we might need him and it wasn't well received.'

Contact with the pathologist was achieved and, with characteristic protest, he agreed to attend at the scene. 'I sometimes think you plan to wreck my weekend, Charles. Yesterday, a suicide, and today—'

Wycliffe interrupted, 'Yes, what about that young man? Any suspicious circumstances?'

'I've a good mind to say you can wait for my report. But I don't suppose it would do any good. He died from cutting his own throat. What more do you want? Do you think somebody else did it for him?'

'I had that in mind as a bare possibility. If he was drugged beforehand.'

'You read too many thrillers, Charles. Forget it. Anyway, about your present offering, I'll be there in under the hour.'

Time to get back to the two women. Wycliffe turned to Kersey. 'I want you with me, Doug. From now on we must play this by the book.'

They were met at the door by Dr Florence and taken to the big room. She had changed into black, a tightly fitting jumper and matching trousers. Presumably the tartan trews had been judged inappropriate for the occasion.

She sat herself on the sofa facing the window with the light accentuating the sharpness of her features. With her page-boy haircut, she reminded Wycliffe of one of those hatchet-faced Lancastrian kings who stare out of the pages of school history books.

Wycliffe said, 'We are in process of recovering from the well a human body wrapped in black plastic. So far, identification has not been attempted, but Dr Franks, the pathologist, will be here shortly and we shall follow the usual procedures. I'm not going to question you at this stage but I have to say that you and your companion will be required to make statements for the record later.'

A quick nervous response that was almost spiteful in tone. 'Isobel is very upset. I doubt if she will be in a condition to make a statement about anything.'

They left it at that. Kersey had said nothing. He was there because from now on caution required that interviews should be monitored.

Outside, Wycliffe said, 'What did you make of her?'

'A cat on a hot tin roof, comes to mind. You didn't insist on seeing Isobel.'

The mortuary men arrived, followed a little later by Franks. The mummy-like figure swathed in black plastic was laid on a sheet spread on the ground near the well. A short length of cord with a loop at the end was attached to the ankles as though the body had been weighted with some object since dislodged.

Franks had taken the temperature of the well water and also a small sample. Now he was bending over the body. 'A midget, Charles.' Franks himself would scarcely have made five-four, but he was rotund.

'If it's Dr Raymond Cross, he was under five foot two and of slight build.'

The police photographer had recorded every stage of the recovery.

Franks said, 'He's wrapped in bin-bags. Not very respectful to the good doctor, but I don't suppose he minded. Anyway, let's get him away.'

'You're not going to remove any of the plastic while you're here?'

'You must be joking, Charles! Have you any idea what we might find underneath?'

The mortuary men carried the body on a stretcher to their van. Franks returned to his Porsche, and it fell to Kersey, with DC Curnow, to accompany the body, maintain continuity of evidence, inform the coroner and generally attend to routine.

Wycliffe and Lucy Lane were left. It was half-past twelve. They returned to the house and once more they were received in the big room by Dr Florence, alone.

She did not wait for Wycliffe to speak. 'I've something to say which doesn't concern Isobel. She is very distressed about Julian's death and she is in her room.'

A pause. Then, boldly, 'You obviously know, or you have guessed, the identity of the body in the well, and for my part, it would be naive to pretend that I didn't know it was there. I want to make a statement.'

She was watching Wycliffe, anxious to gauge the

effect of her words, but he showed no reaction. He said, 'This afternoon, you and your companion will be required to attend for questioning at the police station. The interviews will be recorded, and you will be free to make any statement you wish. You are entitled to have a solicitor present during the interview.'

He turned to Lucy Lane, 'Perhaps you will go to Miss Wilde's room and inform her of the arrangement. It is now a quarter to one; a car will collect you both at three.'

Once more in the yard, getting into the car, Wycliffe said, 'Anywhere around here where we might get a bite of something?'

'I've heard there's a pub-cum-restaurant a mile or so outside the village. We could try it.'

Wycliffe maintained that Lucy could home in on an oasis in the Gobi Desert.

Reflective, Wycliffe decided that being a policeman had much in common with being an actor. You come off stage, leaving tragedy or farce behind, to unwind in the nearest pub.

They found Lucy's eating place in the middle of nowhere with a car-park full of cars. There were tables out of doors but Wycliffe disliked alfresco meals except on picnics, and they settled for a table inside. They ate crab sandwiches and drank coffee, while middle-aged Terrys, Lisas, Jimmys and Sues clustered around the bar, making in-jokes and pretending to be more tipsy than they were.

But the crab was good.

*   *   *

'Interview room number three, sir. The women are already there with DS Lane.'

Wycliffe was uneasy. His main brief had been (and was) to investigate the death of the girl found dead in her car submerged in the quarry pool. The technical and forensic evidence had got him nowhere, and routine police inquiries were bogged down. In this context, the discovery of Dr Raymond's body and Julian's suicide contributed nothing directly, but he believed – that the two women were now psychologically vulnerable.

Interview room number three was quiet as a church. The tiny window overlooked a roundabout which, on weekdays, featured an on-going game of last-across. Now it was deserted.

The two women had elected to be interviewed together and without a solicitor. Dr Florence wore a dress of black and white stripes which hung from her shoulders as from a coat hanger. Isobel, with her pearls, had changed her dress, but not her style.

Lucy, at the tape, said, 'This interview begins at . . . Present . . .'

Wycliffe quoted the gospel according to PACE. 'You are not under arrest . . .'

Then, Dr Florence, impatient with the preliminaries, plunged into her statement.

'It is impossible to convey to a stranger the circumstances in which all this occurred.' She broke off and looked at Wycliffe. 'You must realize that Raymond imposed on Julian, using him both as an object of study and as someone to do the donkey work in connection with his research and writing. Julian, of course, became increasingly resentful. There was constant friction until, finally, Julian's temper got the better of him.'

Dr Florence paused, apparently touched by emotion. 'I returned home one afternoon to find Raymond lying on the floor in the front room. His skull had been fractured by a blow from a bronze ornament that used to stand on the mantelpiece.'

There could be no doubt that she was affected by the scene she described, and there was another break before she added in a low voice, 'Raymond was dead.'

'When was this?'

'It was on February the nineteenth, five years ago. I'm unlikely to forget it.'

She looked from Wycliffe to Lucy, and back again. 'I was in a terrible situation. Julian was horrified by what he had done, but I have to admit that he had my sympathy. Raymond was a man with little sensitivity towards the feelings of others, especially where his work was concerned.

'I had to decide. Whether to allow Julian to be committed to some soulless institution for the foreseeable future, or try to conceal what he had done . . .'

She broke off, and waited, but Wycliffe remained silent so that she was forced to continue. 'I decided that I would report Raymond as a missing person.' She spread her hands. 'And that left me with the awesome task of hiding his body.'

Again she paused for comment or question, but none came.

'I considered the well, but I realized that if the police had the slightest suspicion that the facts were not as I represented them, the well would be investigated.'

She sat back on her chair and let her arms hang limply as though in a posture of surrender.

'Of course I had the advantage of medical knowledge. I wrapped the body in plastic bin-bags, secured them with string, and sealed all the overlapping edges with adhesive tape. That done, with Julian's help, I carried it upstairs and placed it in the large linen-drawer under my bed. It was a bold move, almost foolhardy, but it worked.'

A hint of pride?

She went on, 'I don't need to be told that my conduct was outrageous. In mitigation I can only say that I was conscious of a heavy burden of responsibility for what Julian had been driven to do.'

Yet another fruitless pause for comment that did not come, then, 'The police investigation on the immediate neighbourhood of the house lasted for a week and, as I had foreseen, it included an examination of the well. When I was satisfied that it was over, Julian and I carried the body down and, secured to a large stone, we dropped it into the water. I then spread soil over the capping, and in the following spring I encouraged the growth of brambles and weeds to obscure the well as far as possible.'

She stopped speaking, and by a tired gesture indicated that she had no more to say.

Wycliffe had only two questions, both addressed to Isobel. 'Surely you knew what was happening?'

Isobel's voice was just audible. 'Yes.'

'Do you agree with the account we have just heard?'

'Yes.'

Dr Florence cut in, 'Isobel was deeply shocked by what happened. She took no part in it and it was only out of consideration for Julian that she remained silent.'

Wycliffe ignored the intervention. 'As you know, Julian spoke to me yesterday morning on the telephone. The call came to me at home, through my headquarters, and calls routed in that way are recorded. DS Lane will play the relevant section of the tape.'

A brief interval, then the voice on the tape: 'It's Julian.'

'You want to talk to me?'

'Yes. You must come down . . . It's about Morwenna.'

'Are you speaking from home?'

'Yes . . . You must come down. It was my fault that Morwenna died . . . I told her . . . If only I'd kept quiet she would be here now. But I didn't want more secrets. Not between us. There have been too many in this house.'

Dr Florence sat bolt upright, her bony hands clasped tightly in her lap. Isobel had one hand pressed to her mouth in the manner of a guilty little girl.

Wycliffe's manner was pedantic. 'There is an obvious question. What could Julian have told Morwenna that contributed to her death?'

There was no response from the women and he went on, 'Could it be that he confided the truth about what happened to his adopted father? How he died? And that his body was hidden in the well?'

Both the women remained silent, and Wycliffe addressed the doctor directly. 'Dr Cross?'

Dr Florence spoke with obvious reluctance. 'I suppose so.'

'Miss Wilde?'

'Yes.'

Wycliffe quoted, ' "I told her . . . If only I'd kept quiet she would be here now" – Julian's words. Clearly he had confided to his sister the truth about Dr Raymond's disappearance. Presumably it relieved his mind and he was satisfied that the secret would be safe with her.

'But what if Morwenna was deeply shocked by what she had learned? What if she expressed her repugnance and even threatened exposure?'

The silence in the little room was total. No-one moved. The seconds hand on the wall clock jerked its way once, perhaps twice, around the dial.

Again it was Wycliffe who spoke. 'One has only to ask, who was threatened? And the answer must be the person who killed Dr Raymond. In other words, Julian himself.'

There was a quick intake of breath from Isobel but no-one spoke.

'So we have to believe that on Sunday evening – *last* Sunday evening, Julian attacked his sister, rendering her semi-conscious, carried her to her car, placed her in the passenger seat, drove her to the edge of the quarry, got out, shifted her to the driving seat, strapped her in, then pushed the car over.'

Wycliffe paused, staring at Isobel as though speaking to her alone. Then, in a low voice, he went on, 'So Julian became a murderer for the second time. And this time his victim was the sister it had taken him almost half a lifetime to find.'

Wycliffe stopped speaking and seemed to be waiting. Afterwards, Lucy Lane said that there were little beads of sweat on his forehead.

Suddenly Isobel's voice cut into the silence, strident and compelling. 'I can't take any more of this!'

She turned towards Dr Florence. 'You sit there saying nothing, but you *know* that Julian was no murderer! You know that Julian killed nobody! It was you . . .' Isobel's voice broke, and she added amid sobs, 'Julian killed only himself.'

It seemed for an instant that Dr Florence had not taken in what had been said. Then, suddenly, she sprang to her feet and turned on Isobel, clawing at her face, inarticulate with rage.

Wycliffe lunged across the table and grabbed her arm; Lucy tackled her from behind but she tried to fight them off and it was only with the greatest difficulty that they forced her, still struggling, back into her chair.

It was evening, still Sunday, and the cathedral bells were ringing.

Dr Florence, after a stormy encounter with the medical examiner, was being held for questioning. Wycliffe, Lucy Lane, and Isobel Wilde were back in interview room number three.

Isobel had been treated for minor scratches on her face but now she sat opposite Wycliffe, apparently composed, and in some strange way she seemed older.

When PACE had been placated Wycliffe began to question her.

'You say that Julian was not responsible for the

deaths of Dr Raymond, or of Morwenna. Is that correct?'

'Yes. What she told you about Raymond's death and what she did to conceal it was all true, except that it was she who killed Raymond. Julian was not even in the house at the time . . . I was.'

She was leaning forward in her chair, very pale, hands clenched together. 'And it was I, not Julian, who helped her to do what was done afterwards.'

Wycliffe warned, 'What you are saying could result in you being charged as an accessory to murder and you would be wise to postpone this interview until you are legally represented.'

She said quietly, 'No! . . . No! I'm going through with this now, whatever happens.'

'Very well. You were saying that after Dr Raymond was murdered you assisted in hiding and disposing of his body. Surely Julian must have been aware of all that had happened?'

'Yes, but he took no part in it.'

'So for five years the three of you continued living together, carrying on with your lives, but with this terrible secret between you.'

Isobel started to speak, hesitated, then went ahead. 'I have to say that after the first few weeks it was the best time I had known since I came to Ventonbos. For one thing there was no more quarrelling between Florence and Raymond but there was something else. Until then Julian and I had been properties. He belonged to Raymond and I to Florence. The difference between us was that I was treated kindly – even spoiled, while Julian was little better than a slave to Raymond. With Raymond gone, we both began to feel that we were more part of a family.'

In all his experience Wycliffe could not recall hearing a young woman discussing so calmly and objectively the outcome of a murder.

'Was there an intimate relationship between Florence and you?' The question came from Lucy Lane.

'Oh, yes. I suppose it all centred around that as far as she was concerned.'

'And for you?'

A shrug. 'I think I must have been a late developer. I had nothing to compare it with. Sex was sex. I did what was required of me and I realized that I owed Florence a great deal.'

Wycliffe asked, 'Did things change when Morwenna arrived?'

Isobel frowned. 'Not really. Julian was obsessed by her, but she only came at weekends until that last fortnight.'

'And it was at the end of that fortnight – last Sunday, in fact, that Morwenna died.' Wycliffe spoke slowly and with grave emphasis. 'I need to know a great deal more about that last day. We have been told that Morwenna left in her car at some time between nine and ten o'clock in the morning, and that she did not return. That is not true, is it?'

There was a long pause before Isobel said in a voice that was barely audible, 'No . . . No, it is not. It was quite early when she left and for some reason that I didn't understand Julian seemed very upset. He was mooning around, wandering in and out of the house. Florence was still in bed. In the end he came into the kitchen where I was washing a few things in the sink and stood there for a while, watching me.

'Finally he said, "I told her about Raymond. I felt that I had to. I mean, she's my sister. But she's terribly upset. I've never seen her like it before. She said that she had to get away to think." '

Isobel sighed. 'Of course I had to tell Florence, and she was horrified.'

There was an interval before she went on, 'Morwenna came back in the late evening and she and Florence spent a long time together in her room. What happened there I don't know, but when Florence came down she said that Morwenna had been much more understanding and that she had settled down for the night and didn't want to be disturbed.

'I asked about Julian and she said that she'd given him a sedative and he was sleeping. She did that sometimes when he'd worked himself up into a state.'

Isobel asked for a glass of water and the tape was interrupted while it was provided. She sat back in her chair and after several sips indicated that she was ready to continue.

'In the end I went to bed and I must have slept, though I seemed to be half aware that something was going on. Suddenly I was wide awake. My room is at the back of the house overlooking the yard. I could hear movement. I got out to see what was happening. Sometimes there are foxes.'

She paused, perhaps troubled by the images she was now to recall. 'I saw Florence, and she was carrying Morwenna on her back . . . Morwenna's body was limp and I thought that she must be dead.'

'She was *carrying* Morwenna?'

'Oh, yes. Florence is very strong. She carried Raymond's body upstairs to her room where she hid it until the police had gone. I saw her do it. She needed no help then.

'Morwenna's Mini was there with the passenger door open and she just slid the body into the passenger seat, strapped it in, got in herself, and drove off.'

Wycliffe said, 'I thought she had given up driving after an accident.'

Isobel was dismissive. 'Florence drove well enough when it suited her.'

Outside the sky had clouded over and there were streaks of rain on the little window.

Isobel said, 'I sat there for what seemed to be hours, watching for her, and there was light in the sky when she finally came back – walking.'

The silence lasted so long that Wycliffe prompted, 'And in the morning?'

'We were told that Morwenna had left in the night without a word. A little later she said, "If there are ever any questions about Morwenna leaving I think we should say that she went off quite early on Sunday morning and that we did not see her again." '

Lucy Lane said, 'And you went along with that, both of you!'

Isobel was stung. 'You don't understand! You've no idea what it was like! We were totally dependent – both of us!' She broke off and there were tears in her eyes. 'Anyway, it's over now. Do what you like.'

Chapter Fourteen

Sunday August 20 (continued)

Wycliffe slept at home that night. Slept is a euphemism. For much of the night he lay pondering over and troubled by what was probably the most disturbing case of his career. In some ways it was not so much a case as an experience. And a salutary one.

As far as he was concerned it began with a missing girl, but the real beginning, many years before, must surely have been the unwanted pregnancy of another girl, a girl of sound lower-middle-class stock, in love with an ambitious youth who had scarcely a penny to his name. Traditionally the very stuff of romance, but not in this case.

The discreet delivery of a crippled child and its adoption by an ideal couple tidied up the whole episode nicely. Or seemed to.

A dispute over land rights, and the bookseller, Meagor, came into the picture. What was Lucy's assessment? 'Weak but dangerously honest.' And his honesty landed him in trouble.

It was a tortuous path which led to Ventonbos. The young man who had been born an illegitimate cripple was a disciple of Lewis Carroll, but he lived in a world with characters that were more truly menacing than any encountered by Alice.

The alarm went off at seven. Helen raised herself on one elbow and looked down at him. 'You're not really fit.'

'I'll make up for it later. We'll have a few days off.'

And Helen said, 'Yes; those elusive few days.'

Two months later

An October day with a blustery wind blowing fine rain before it. Wycliffe was in Falmouth and his sense of decency required that he should call on the bookseller.

The shop looked as he had first known it. The broken windows had been replaced and the graffiti scrubbed from the walls.

The bell pinged as usual and he was inside; uncertain of his reception.

Footsteps, and Meagor arrived. 'Mr Wycliffe!'

The ritual response came to his lips and the words were spoken before he realized it, 'I don't suppose you have anything for me?'

'I think I may have. It came in last week and I thought of you then. It's a copy of Charles Henderson's *History of Cornwall*. In nice condition.'

He followed Meagor down one of the aisles between the bookshelves. In the office space at the back a girl was seated at the table that had been Morwenna's. She was making entries in a ledger as Morwenna had done, and a shaft of light from the rain-streaked window shone on her blonde hair.

'This is Becky, my daughter, Mr Wycliffe. She has

decided to give up the law, at least for the time being, and come into the book business. I don't know where I should be without her.'

The girl looked up, and Wycliffe received a momentary glance from her blue eyes before she returned to her work. Had her lips moved in a murmured greeting?

Embarrassed, Meagor said, 'I'll get the Henderson.'

THE END